Black Horse, Black Rider

Wither goest thou like wind across the moors?
Stallion black as Hell.
White mane streaming like spume
From ocean's green wave.
Wild freedom whistles past your ears.
No bit nor rein dost hold you back,
Nor spur you on.

Wither goest thou like wind across the moors,
Rider straight from Hell?
Eyes flashing like hot red coals
From the devil's own furnace hearth.
War's dying screams still linger in your ears.
No man nor God dost stay your hand,
But vengeance spurs you on.

Wither goest thou like wind across the moors?
Horse, Rider – yet as one.
Fleeing like wraiths towards your destiny.
No mercy can lessen your pace,
Nor humanity soften your heart.
Death spurs you on.

BLACK HORSE, BLACK RIDER

D. Forrester Newhall

Fireside Publications
Lady Lake, Florida

Fireside Publications
1004 San Felipe Lane
Lady Lake, Florida
www.firesidepubs.com

ISBN: 978-1-935517-61-0

Cover Photo by Abramova Kseniya
Curtesy of shutterstock.com

Acknowledgements

In Chapters II and VII I have used endearing terms in a Russian Gypsy dialect. I have written them phonetically along with the words to the songs *Dve Gitari* (Two Guitars) and *Dyeni Noch* (Day and Night).

The Russian words in the text are by the kind permission of Theodore Bikel. Mr. Bikel wrote, "The language is Russian Gypsy, which is not, strictly speaking, Romany. It is a dialect peculiar to the Russian Gypsies. I did not write the words, but did try to write them phonetically as accurately as possible. Gypsies are guilty of slurring words and syllables often in an arbitrary manner that varies each time they sing the song. The words are original with the Gypsies." These and many other songs can be heard on Bikel's album "Songs of a Russian Gypsy," recorded by Elektra.

My special thanks to Omah Kiser who spent many long hours proofreading the manuscript.

(Due to special circumstances, the manuscript has since been revised and re-edited.)

iii

Black Horse, Black Rider has been edited and published in memory of the author, Diana Harned, writing as D. Forrester Newhall, by her good friends, Joan and Glen L. West. During Diana's lifetime, Glen spent many hours editing and advising her in the writing of the first two novels of this trilogy:

The Hunt is Away

The Spider's Web

Chapter I

Winter had begun to show itself over the rugged Scottish highlands. In the lower area of the forest, most of the multicolored leaves had fallen; only a few stubborn ones still clung tenaciously to cold bare branches. Patches of frost appeared in the hollows of the moor where in its hurry south the weakened sun had failed to penetrate.

The destination of the three men in the silver gray sedan loomed ahead of them through the mist. Jim, the driver, swept the car through the wrought iron gates set in grey fieldstone pillars. From the back seat he shared with his older companion, Henri Bolkonsky's first sight of Lothian Academy was forbidding. And this was where he would spend the next few months in hiding from a group of ex-Nazis intent on assassinating him to prevent him from testifying against their friends at the Nuremburg Trials.

Jim pulled the car up to the door of the administration building, an early Nineteenth Century structure dominating the rectangular parade ground that lay before it. Henri stepped out of the car, his eyes slowly sweeping the campus. A mass of gray lay before him. Old gray stone buildings stood starkly against the leaden gray sky and mullioned windows reflected blank stares back to him. Two Twelfth Century crenellated towers flanked the administration building, ancient trees stretching out toward the four dormitories that stood opposite each other on either side of the parade ground. Smaller buildings ranged behind the major structures and a few men walked along the paths, as gusts of chill wind swept across the campus and tugged at the hems of their gray woolen capes. A high wall on the fourth side, pierced by the great gates through which the three men had just entered, enclosed the quadrangle.

3

Major Robert Herring had gotten out of the car and stood next to Henri. "A bit on the dour side, but a nice setting," Henri remarked quietly.

"A typical understatement." Bob grinned. "Come on, we had better go up to General Dayton's office first. He's expecting us and we're late."

The two men started up the path, Henri moving softly, tense and cautious as he always was in a new place, his eyes taking in everything. He would settle down when he grew familiar with his new surroundings, but now he was like a cat exploring new territory. Bob, knowing his friend, kept up a stream of light-hearted conversation, to which Henri only half listened until they entered the outer room of the general's office. Henri stood just inside the door sizing up the few people in the room before moving forward at Bob's side.

Bob and Henri introduced themselves to the general's aide. The aide saluted and nodded. "Wait here a moment, sir," he said. He left the room, but returned only moments later to escort them into the general's private office.

As the two men entered, General Dayton closed the dossier lying open on his desk and stood, extending his hand to Henri. "Glad to meet you, Bolkonsky," and turning to Bob, "At ease, Major, please sit down gentlemen." Henri smiled diffidently and settled his trim six foot plus body in a comfortable chair.

Of medium height, with pepper and salt hair receding from a high forehead, General Dayton's movements were as quick, decisive and economic as his speech. Looking much younger than his fifty-three years, his army career which had followed that of his father and grandfather showed in his manner and bearing. To his troops he had been known as a terror, but had also been liked and respected by them. Now as he sat back in his chair looking over this man new to the Academy, he said quietly, "It appears you have special permission to enter our Academy, Bolkonsky. Since I was given only the bare essentials before your arrival, perhaps you can explain it."

"I think Major Herring can explain the reason better than I, sir," Henri replied, quietly tossing the ball to Bob, giving himself more time to study the man in front of him.

4

General Dayton turned his level gaze toward Bob, one eyebrow raised. "Mr. Bolkonsky is due to testify at the Nuremberg trials. There are a group of ex-S.S. officers who want to stop him before he gets there. We have his written depositions and tapes of his testimony, but it is important that he appear in person. We felt the safest place he could be without completely restricting his freedom was here at this Academy."

"I see. Why here in particular, Mr. Bolkonsky? Why not another school or University?"

It was Henri's turn to meet Dayton's sharp eyes. "Major Herring actually picked it. He told me you needed an assistant to teach Military Intelligence for one thing and that I could at the same time finish University here. I also know this part of Scotland well as I trained with the S.O.E. nearby. Above all, I do not want my family harmed and as long as I am not with them they will be safe." He smiled slightly. "Also, members of my family have been in the army, or rather in the cavalry, for generations."

The general studied the young man for a few moments. Late twenties, he guessed. He was impressed with Bolkonsky's blond good looks, but even more so with his proud bearing; his soft-spoken voice with its quiet note of command, the level gaze of his dark blue eyes. "You will have to abide by the rules and regulations…no special privileges."

A quick smile pulled at the corners of Henri's lips. "I expect that, sir."

General Dayton pressed a buzzer on his desk, "Tell Mr. McGovern to come in, please." Then turning to Henri, he went on, "You will room with Mr. McGovern and Mr. Forrest. McGovern will show you around and explain the procedures to you." The general glanced up as McGovern stood at attention in front of him. "At ease, McGovern, this is Henri Bolkonsky. He is assigned to your room. See to it he is shown the ropes."

"Yes sir." Peter McGovern and Henri eyed each other carefully as Henri rose to shake hands.

"Why don't you wait outside while I talk with General Dayton for a few minutes, Henri?" Bob said. Henri nodded, saluted the general, and followed Pete McGovern out of the room.

After the two men had left, Bob turned to Dayton, "There are a few restrictions concerning Mr. Bolkonsky. First, he is not to leave the campus alone at any time. He must always be with a group of four to six. This is a precaution against his getting picked off easily by a sniper or for a kidnap attempt."

"I understand." The general nodded.

"Secondly, medically speaking, he is not up to par yet. His shoulder is still in bad condition and so is his left leg. He is to do no strenuous sports or exercise until he is completely well."

"I read an abbreviated note in his dossier, something to do with the Communists in Austria. What exactly happened to him?" Dayton asked.

"Because of Henri's knowledge of British and American intelligence agents on the Continent during and after the war, the Communists wanted to get their hands on him nearly as badly as the Nazis do now. The only exception was the Communists wanted him alive—the Nazis want him dead. About two months ago in Vienna on the border between the Russian and American Zones, while he was escaping from the Communists, he was shot up badly. Because of his previous history, he does not heal quickly and you have to watch him."

"Dr. White will give him a complete physical today and tell me what he is allowed to do. I've read part of his dossier and understand what you mean. Anything else?"

"From his dossier you will note he does not look for trouble, but he will not avoid it either. He will take risks, calculated ones, but risks all the same. We need him alive," Herring said flatly.

"I understand. We'll see to it he is delivered to you alive and in better condition than he is now."

Bob rose smiling. "That I would like to see. Thank you, sir, for co-operating with us."

"Not at all. He is the type of man I like to see here at the Academy. I hope to convince him to continue on even after the trials. He has a fine record." The general rose too and held out his hand, "Goodbye, Major."

While Bob and the general talked, Pete McGovern and Henri were becoming acquainted in the outer room. A tall, long-limbed man, Pete was built like the halfback he had been in high school. No amount of cutting, brushing or slicking would ever keep his sandy red hair—his most outstanding feature—under control. Lively blue eyes that appeared as innocent as a child's, looked out from his open, friendly face. Under his tan could be seen the freckles that went with the red hair. A good six feet tall, in breath and weight, he could make two of Henri. His wide and generous mouth turned up at the corners.

Henri stood casually with one hand in his trouser pocket, a half smile on his face, his six feet three inch lean frame seemingly relaxed. The two men had remained silent for a minute after leaving the general's presence, studying each other quietly. Finally Henri broke the silence, "You are American but I can't quite place your accent. Where do you come from?"

"Texas," Pete said smiling. "It's not as thick now as it used to be. My dad says he reckons I'm becoming Europeanized."

"I've heard a lot about Texas. What part do you come from?"

"Near Dallas, a little town called Bluff." Pete shrugged. "No one has ever heard of it."

Henri's eyes sharpened, his mind going back to a burning plane in Southern France and a co-pilot from Bluff, Texas whom he had pulled free. The man's name was Dave McGovern. He and the rest of the crew had spent some time in hiding with Henri and his men before getting back to England. Now Henri asked, "Do you live on a ranch?"

"I don't know why everyone seems to think anyone from Texas must live on a ranch." Pete laughed. "Actually, I do. It's a nice little spread."

Henri grinned, "Traditionally, anyone from Texas is an oil millionaire or a cattle baron, carries a six shooter, wears boots and a Stetson and plays a guitar. Do you have any brothers or sisters?"

"Um hum, a brother older than I...Dave. He more or less runs the ranch now with Dad." Pete watched the half smile playing around Henri's lips and asked," Where are you from?"

7

"Europe in general." Henri grinned at the puzzled look on Pete's face, and went on to explain, "Actually, I was born in Stockholm, Sweden, but have lived all over Europe most of my life."

Bob came out of the general's office. "Okay, everything is set. Let's go."

When the men got to the car where Jim waited, Bob turned to Henri, "Be careful and take care of yourself." Henri gave him a wry grin and nodded. "If you need help, Jim will be at the Royal Hotel in Fort William."

"Right. What's the telephone number?"

"It's 2681, room 7. Got it?"

"Yeah."

"I'll be there or at the local police station. Their number is 4872."

"Right."

"Any questions?" Bob asked.

Henri was about to say something, but glanced in McGovern's direction, changed his mind and shook his head. As Jim was about to pull away, Bob said, "Remember Jim is close by. Call him."

Henri watched with a speculative look in his eyes as the car drove off.

Pete had been watching and listening curiously to the three men, but decided not to ask any questions at the moment; something in Henri's manner stopped him. Instead, he said, "Let's get you outfitted and then I'll show you the room and after that you can go for your physical."

Henri nodded his agreement, picked up his suitcase and walked beside his new roommate.

"Hey Pete, where's the new guy?" Vance dropped his books on the table.

"Over having his physical."

"What's he like?"

"He seems okay, but he's not much of a talker. He sure learns fast though. When I told him the rules and regulations, he

8

seemed to have them memorized almost as soon as I got them out of my mouth."

"Where's he from?"

"He was born in Sweden."

"Where did he go to school?"

"Don't know."

"Did he tell you about his family? Does he have a sister?"

"I don't know."

"Well, don't you know anything about him other than where he was born?" Vance asked in exasperation.

"I said he didn't talk much. Except for asking me some questions about where I came from and my family, he kept the conversation strictly on Academy matters. He seemed to have deliberately raised a barrier." Pete paused for a minute frowning. "You know that guy really puzzles me."

"Why?"

"When we walked across the quad, he stopped dead in his tracks and turned a full circle scanning the hills, Ben Nevis Loch and Mamore Forest with a funny look in his eyes; then he asked where all the paths led and about the loch and cliffs."

"Why is that so puzzling? He's probably curious about the area and how to get places."

"No. It was more than that." Pete shrugged. "I can't explain it. It was as if, well, as if he expected to be attacked and wanted to know the best excape routes."

Vance laughed. "Now you *are* letting your imagination run away with you."

"But why is he allowed, against all the rules, to start in the middle of the term? Then, it's his whole attitude and that cryptic conversation with the two guys who brought him here."

"Look, Pete," Vance put his hand on Pete's shoulder. "We'll find out this evening after dinner. The guy is probably just shy and needs a little encouragement."

Henri walked into the room and the conversation stopped.

The room Henri shared with Pete McGovern and Vance Forrest was only slightly larger and a little less Spartan than the cell he had occupied a few weeks earlier. This room held three beds, a table which served all of them as a desk, three chairs, three footlockers, which served as dressers and three steel lockers for hanging their clothes. The only light in the room other than that coming from the window, emanated from a shaded lamp hanging from the ceiling directly over the table. Henri had been leafing through his books trying to find out how far behind he was when a bell rang; almost immediately the door opened and a young man stuck his head into the room. "Hey Pete, time to finish that chess game."

Pete looked up from his books, "Okay. I'll be right with you." The head disappeared. "Come on Henri, you can finish that later." Closing their books and stacking them neatly on the table the three men headed for the door.

Vance, Pete and Henri walked into the recreation room, by now crowded with men. Henri had learned that each dormitory held men from all of the three classes. First year men were quartered on the top floor of one dormitory, second year men on the second and third year men on the first floor. The ground floor held the O.D.'s office, a study room and a recreation room. Fourth year men had a dormitory to themselves.

Henri stood quietly by the door and glanced quickly around. He saw a relatively large room, nearly square shaped, with groups of worn overstuffed chairs, battered tables and couches scattered around. A table tennis table stood at one end of the room and in a fireplace, halfway along the wall opposite him, a fire burned. Faded prints of the Academy and pictures of some of its more illustrious graduates hung on cream colored walls. The room was warm, smoke eddying here and there from pipes or cigarettes. He noticed someone had opened a window at the far end. Everyone seemed to be talking at once with shouts of laughter rising above the din. He could discern American accents mixed with English, Scottish and Irish.

"Come on, Henri, over here," Pete said touching his arm and pointing to some empty chairs. Settling the three of them in front of the fireplace, Pete decided not to approach Henri with direct questions. "We were talking about accents earlier today. Yours isn't Swedish and it isn't wholly English either. I can't quite place it."

10

"I was born in Stockholm, but lived most of my life in France and Germany." A small smile quirked up the corner of Henri's mouth as he added, "I'm also multilingual, so my accent is really a combination of tongues."

"But your name is what? Polish? Hungarian? Russian?" Vance asked.

"Russian. My mother was American and my father Russian, educated at Oxford."

"How long have you been in England?" Pete asked forgetting he hadn't planned to ask direct questions.

"About a month."

Pete raised an eyebrow. "And before that?"

"As I said, on the Continent."

"Then; you were on the Continent when the war broke out?" Vance asked.

"Yes." Henri nodded, adding, "I was in France when the Nazis walked in."

"Where did you spend the war years?" Pete asked.

"Mostly in France and Germany." A half smile played around Henri's lips as he answered this barrage of questions. He was struck by the open honest curiosity of the Americans, so different from the reticent Europeans.

"It must have been pretty tough over there," Pete said quietly. "I heard from my brother, Dave that food was extremely scarce and a lot of people starved, to say nothing of the nice things the Nazis were doing."

Henri shrugged. "It certainly was not easy, but then there was always the black market. You could get anything you wanted if you could pay the price and were willing to go that route."

"I would like to go back again before heading for the States," Vance remarked.

Henri glanced at him sharply, "When were you there?"

"During the war. I was a commando," he said quietly.

"Where did you operate?" Henri studied Vance with new interest.

"Mostly North Africa, but also in Italy and France."

Henri and Vance started to talk about the North African campaign and about commando raids they both had heard about or

11

had been on. Pete sat back listening, watching his new roommate while several other men in the room came over to listen. Vance and Henri were arguing the relative merits of Montgomery, Rommel, Eisenhower and Patton, with Henri favoring Rommel and Patton for their brilliant daring, drive and ability to take risks. He and Vance used chessmen to set up various battles to prove their points. Vance looked up and stopped in mid-sentence. Henri glanced up too. Slowly, a smile spread over his face as he rose, "John Stanley," he said. "It's been a long time."

"I don't believe it," Stanley's voice came in musing amazement then he almost shouted, "Good God where the hell did you come from?"

"Oh! I always turn up one way or another," Henri said.

Stanley grabbed Henri's shoulders making him nearly keel over. Henri grabbed John's wrist, turned away, closed his eyes for a minute against the pain that raced through him. "Why the bloody hell do you Yanks have to be so enthusiastic?" he said with a tight laugh in his voice. "Take is easy; my shoulder cannot take more punishment."

"Sorry, Henri. Are you all right? What happened?" Stanley looked worried, one hand on Henri's arm, the other on his right shoulder, steadying him.

"Ja. I am all right," he answered, his voice still tight.

Stanley looked quickly away, the worried look still in his eyes, and called over his shoulder, "Hey, Larry, look who turned up out of the blue!"

Larry Parker, a tall, dark haired man, walked across the room, a broad grin on his face, his eyes dancing, "My God, it's good to see you again!"

Henri dodged the hand coming down on his left shoulder, shaking his head. "Watch out, that shoulder hasn't fully recovered. Glad to see you Larry!"

"What happened?" John asked, a frown on his face.

"Oh, I had a little dust-up with the Russians about a month ago. Our side won, but I caught a couple of bullets. What are you two doing here of all places? I thought both of you were heading back for the States as soon as the war was over."

Larry pulled himself up to his full six feet, clicked his heels and bowed, saying in a mock serious tone with a mock English accent, "We are learning to be officers and gentlemen. Besides, he added, a little sheepishly, "I found a little London girl one night in an air raid shelter and I've grown quite fond of her."

Henri laughed. "I feel sorry for the Academy, but your English girl is very lucky indeed."

Larry and John glanced at each other and laughed too, both remembering some wild escapades they had experienced with Henri on several commando raids that would have horrified any Academy graduate. "What about you? What are you doing here?"

"The same. How long have you two been here?"

"We're in our second year," John replied, "and therefore are your superior officers." His eyes held amusement. "So you will have to show a little respect, old man."

"Yes, sir!" Henri grinned, for on the raids they had been on together, his specialized knowledge of the country and language had made him the superior officer, though in actual fact, he held no rank at all. The three had become close friends, respecting each others' abilities during those times of shared danger, and a mutual trust had grown quickly among them. Now Henri asked, "Do you know Vance Forrest? He was a commando too; North Africa, Italy and France."

"Oh, yes. Most of us old pros have gotten together," Larry acknowledged Vance with a nod, but immediately turned back to Henri. "By the way, welcome to the Academy, glad you showed up."

A bell rang as they were about to sit down and the room began to clear. "Damn, lights out." Larry looked disappointed.

"We'll see you tomorrow night, Henri. We can talk then." John said.

Everyone dispersed to their various rooms and to bed. Henri lay in the dark thinking, and relaxed for the first time that day. He was glad Stanley and Parker were there. It was going to make it a lot easier for him. He was also glad Forrest was his roommate. If things became really sticky, these three would understand and know how to react quickly.

Chapter Two

At ease, Bolkonsky. Sit down." General Dayton leaned back in his chair frowning slightly. "You've been here a month now. How are things going?"

"Fairly well, sir. I'm beginning to settle into the routine." Henri kept his face and eyes a mask

"You've been doing a lot of exploring, I hear."

I wonder what this is all about? "Yes, sir. I know all the entrances and exits to the Academy, the most dangerous spots for me on campus and most of the forest paths nearest here and the Loch."

"Good. How are your studies coming along?"

"I'm almost caught up, sir. McGovern, Forrest and I have worked out an arrangement whereby they help me in those subjects in which I'm behind and I help them in their languages, military strategy and intelligence."

"Good. Then you're making friends here."

"Some," Henri answered evasively. When Dayton raised an eyebrow, he went on, "I've been kept busy with my studies and the tutoring, so I haven't had much extra time."

"Have you met any of the former commandos we have here?"

"Yes, sir. A couple I knew from the war and several others they've introduced me to."

"And, how is the tutorial class going?"

"Very well, sir. I've been asked to take on another group, third year men who are somewhat in advance of their class."

"How do you find them?"

"They are extremely bright and intelligent, sir, and I enjoy tutoring them." Henri smiled. "They certainly make me work to keep ahead of them and pounce instantly if I hesitate in giving them an answer."

"You've had a spot of trouble with one or two of them, I understand."

So that's it! "Well, yes…in a way, sir, but I feel they were only testing me to see how much they could get away with."

He wondered if the general knew of the incident that particularly had disturbed the tranquility of his first month. One day, an old German newspaper clipping with a picture of Heinrich von Spieldau, Count of Fruchtsam, had appeared on his desk. The article accompanying the picture stated that von Spieldau, a lieutenant in the Wehrmacht, had just become an aide to General von Graf and that at Berchtesgarten the Fuhrer had awarded the Iron Cross First Class for exceptional bravery on the Russian Front to the lieutenant along with a promotion to Captain. The name was van Spieldau, but the man in the photograph was unmistakably Henri.

When Henri had walked into the classroom, he had noticed the newspaper lying on his desk, had simply put it to one side without comment or change in his expression and conducted the class as usual.

"They aren't giving you any trouble in class now?"

"No, sir," Henri replied, but thought to himself, *not in class.* He had crossed swords several times with three of them. In front of everyone at the rifle range one day, he had lashed into them verbally for being careless with their weapons. An undeclared state of hostilities now existed between them.

"I see. All right. How are your shoulder and leg holding up?"

"Quite well, sir."

"You've been riding and fencing, I understand."

"Yes, sir. Fortunately, the doctor has let me do both. Apparently, I've made some progress, for today he is letting me begin gymnastics. In fact, I'm due at the gym in a few minutes, sir."

"All right, I'll let you go." Dayton rose. "I'm glad to hear you're doing so well, Bolkonsky, but don't overdo it." He smiled, then added with a slight frown, "If you run into any serious problems that door is always open."

15

"Thank you, sir." Henri saluted, bowed slightly and left the room quickly.

Working out in the gym with his instructor, Colonel Grey, a rusty Henri began to get the feel of timing and movement again. After an hour, Grey called a halt. "It's time we quit, Bolkonsky. We'll work out again tomorrow."

"But, I'm not tired, sir."

"The doctor ordered me not to let you go on too long at first. Don't push so hard. You'll catch up in time and there's no hurry. I like working with you, Henri. You have beautiful co-ordination and control, and lots of determination. Those are qualities I admire in a man, but right now, take it easy."

"Thank you, sir. I appreciate your confidence, but may I just practice a little alone?"

"As long as you don't stay at it too long. Lock the door when you leave." Colonel Grey watched him for a few minutes, then left.

Henri worked out for another half hour before begining to tire. He wiped his face with the towel around his neck and started for the showers, but turned at a sound behind him. "Colonel Grey has..." he began. His three antagonists faced him. Their cold eyes and grim faces told him he was in trouble. *Bloody hell! I'm no match for any one of them right now, let alone all three! I could stave off the inevitable for a short time, but they'll overpower me ...unless I can get to a weapon...*

"We warned you never to get caught alone or we would beat the hell out of you. Now your time has come, Bolkonsky."

Slowly, Henri began to back toward a row of sabers hanging on the wall, hoping to get to one before they rushed him. The three men started to move in as his groping hand closed over the hilt of the nearest saber. Henri lifted it and swung it in an arc, forcing the three to leap back. Carefully, he moved toward the outside door, keeping his back to the wall. The men kept pace with him, moving in on one side or the other.

Suddenly, one broke away, grabbed a long pole and began to parry the swing of Henri's saber. Another ducked under his guard and hit his injured shoulder with a hard right, momentarily stunning him as a vicious streak of pain raced through his side, The third man twisted his left arm in a hammerlock, while the second man slammed his fist into Henri's midriff. Henri doubled over now fighting for breath, weakly trying to break away. Quickly, one of his tormentors stepped in and grabbed his other arm, pinning him down. Blows rained into his body, his knees buckled under him and he mercifully passed out.

The men dragged him across the floor and down a flight of stairs. There the beating continued, only now the three took turns. Through a haze, as if from a long distance, he heard a harsh voice repeating over and over again, "You thought you were the master race you damned Nazi. You deserve worse than this. We'll teach you, you arrogant bastard. God damn you." Finally, they dropped him to the floor and left him there.

When Henri came to, a faint glow from the furnace told him he was in the basement of the gym. He had no idea how long he had been there. The rough concrete floor rubbed against his cheek and hands as he tried to drag himself to his knees. Black waves of nausea swept over him leaving an acrid taste in his mouth, making him nearly faint again. Slowly, he crawled to the stairs, guided by the glow from the furnace; his body feeling like a mass of jelly, his muscles screaming in protest at every movement. Painfully, he dragged himself up, using the railing, collapsing several times on the way.

The gym was in full swing, men exercising, lifting weights, and running on the track. Seeing Henri staggering through the door, his face covered with dried blood, Larry stopped dead. He leapt forward and caught Henri just before he fell. "Holy hell! One of you guys help me get him into the gym," Larry yelled, half carrying, half dragging his friend into the room and laying him on a mat. "Get the doctor and an ambulance!" He checked Henri's pulse and began to check for broken bones. A small group gathered around them as someone brought a blanket, laying it over Henri's inert body. Slowly, Henri's eyes opened, he looked around, vaguely at first, but as his vision cleared, he recognized Larry.

"Who did this to you, Henri?"

Henri only closed his eyes again before whispering painfully, "There were three of them."

"Who? I'll kill the bastards!"

"No! No you will not. They…are mine…and I…will take care of them."

Doctor White hurried in and bent over Henri. He asked a few short questions, picked up a needle and filled it. Henri, weak as he was, caught the doctor's wrist, his eyes cold, "I do not like needles, doctor."

"This will only ease the pain and let us move you more easily."

"I would rather take my chances without it," Henri said through clenched teeth, having witnessed times when needles held other than pain killing medicines.

The two glared at each other, wills clashing. Doctor White finally shrugged his shoulders and nodded. With a sign, two assistants started to move Henri onto the stretcher. Henri bit back a cry, his body arching in pain, and passed out again. The doctor shook his head and quickly gave Henri the prepared injection.

Val Cranston, the O.D. on duty, stuck his head into the room, "Hey, Bolkonsky, you've got a phone call."

Henri glanced up and winced. Still stiff from the beating, when he moved too quickly in the wrong direction, his muscles protested loudly. With effort, he rose and followed Val to his office and lifted the receiver lying off its hook on the desk. "Hello, Bolkonsky here."

"Is this Henri Stephenovich Bolkonsky?" a distant hoarse voice asked.

"Yes, it is. Who's speaking?" The line went dead. Henri clicked the hook up and down a couple of times before hanging up, his eyes thoughtful.

"Get cut off?" Val asked, looking up from the book he was reading.

"Yes. Did you get his name?"

"No, sorry. I didn't."

The telephone ran again. Henri hesitated and then picked up the receiver. "Hello."

"Henri, is that you?" His uncle's voice was unmistakable.

"Yes. How are you?" Henri sat on the edge of the desk, smiling. "No, I'm fine, just studying hard—Everything here is fine—Yes, I'm just about caught up—Good, yes, put Maman on— Maman, how are you?—Yes, the doctor is pleased. The shoulder has healed nicely and my leg is much better. As a matter of fact, I'm doing so well I've started doing gymnastics again—Good. No, everything is going smoothly and I'm getting along well. Do stop worrying, ma belle. You are like a mother hen with one chick— Yes, Maman, I promise I will write. How is Maria?—Good. Give her my love—and Philippe?—I miss them both—Yes, please put Uncle Paul back on.

"Uncle Paul, is everything all right? No untoward incidents or anything? No strangers loitering about the place?—No? Good. By the way, did you call a few minutes ago?—No? Well, someone did but we got cut off. If it was important they'll call back. Give my love to the family—right. Goodbye."

Henri's hand was still on the receiver when the phone rang again. It was Jim, and Henri's face was grim as he spoke with him. "Did you call a few minutes ago?—No, it was not my family—No, the men who beat me up were from the Academy and completely outside the other thing. They're red herrings, I'm sure of that—Oh, come off it, Jim, I can't carry a gun in this uniform; besides it wouldn't do any good against a rifle—I do carry a knife—yes, strapped to my wrist—There are only three dangerous spots on campus and I avoid them—Right. Tell Bob about it—Fine. Goodnight."

"May I ask what that was about?"

"There is a game known as 'Fox and Hounds.' The object of the game is to see which can be the more clever, the fox or the hound." Henri leaned against the doorframe, his hands in his pockets. "The fox runs and the hound follows its scent. When the fox runs for cover, it is the hound's job to find him. But if the fox is very clever, he can take on protective coloring and elude the hound. And, if he is a very, very clever fox, he can also turn the game around when the need arises. In other words, the hunted becomes the hunter and that is when the hound must watch out."

Val sat with his chin on his hand listening to this bit of nonsense. He knew Henri well enough to know there was a hidden meaning behind all this, but he wasn't quite sure what it was. "I see, and which are you, a fox or a hound?"

"You catch on quickly, a fox, but sometimes a hound."

"And who are the hounds?"

"Sometimes European foxhounds and sometimes English foxhounds."

"And the foxes…"

"Oh, they can be silver foxes that move only in the shadows of the night, or red foxes that move in daylight or even white Russian foxes who can do both.

"All right, Henri. It's almost time for lights out."

Henri grinned as he left the office and climbed the stairs to his room. He undressed and slipped into bed, but as he lay in the dark, his mind kept turning back to the mysterious call and his conversation with Jim. He sensed danger and he would rely on his instincts to deal with it. They had never let him down. However, even though convinced the attack on him made by the three men in his class was completely separate from the "other thing;" he was not one to let such an assault go unpunished.

During the next month, Henri carried on as if nothing had happened. He didn't let his three antagonists know he was watching them, biding his time until he felt strong enough to take his revenge.

The men were worthy opponents. Mario Leonardo held the boxing championship of the Academy; his sparring partner and roommate, Steve Velp, held the runner-up position; and his third roommate, Burt Ferranto, held the wrestling championship. Hatred of Henri seethed within each.

Assessing the situation, Henri knew the three men, though all shorter than he, outweighed him by over three and a half stone and they were in top shape. He counted on his fast reflexes, perfect co-ordination and, above all, his extensive training by the British Commandos, to win the fight. He had only to wait for an appropriate time to challenge them.

Mario was scheduled to fight the champion from their rival academy in Ireland on Saturday. Henri made it a point to watch Steve and Mario as they worked out in the gym in preparation. Nothing missed his eyes as they sparred while he put the finishing touches on his own planned strategy.

During the middle of the week following Mario's victory over his Irish opponent, the opportunity presented itself. Henri's last class of the day had finished. He stood on the steps of their dormitory talking to Vince and Pete, when Mario, Steve and Burt came striding out the door, and just behind them were Henri's two war buddies, John Stanley and Larry Parker with Val Handly, the O.D.

"I say, Larry, what did you think of the fight Saturday?"

"It was a really good one. Mario was sure in good form."

Henri's voice held a deliberate sneer. "I don't think so. He was just lucky. The Irishman was a far more skillful fighter. Too bad he wasn't up to par. He would have sent Mario to the floor by the third round if he had been."

His three friends reached his side and the six men stood in a small group. Henri's voice, though quiet, carried far enough for Mario to hear. Henri didn't look directly at him, but was aware the three men were listening intently.

"For God's sake, keep your voice down, Henri. Mario is standing right over there," Vance said.

"I know. I could take him on and beat him to the canvas easily. Mario is no real fighter; he doesn't have the stomach for it and his buddies, Burt and Steve, are even worse than he is."

Vance put his hand on Henri's arm, but Henri continued, "Did you notice the way Mario kept pulling his punches and backing away from the Irishman? He acted as if he were afraid of him. It was pure luck that he landed any punches at all. How he or any of them became champions here is beyond me!"

Burt started over in their direction while the men around Henri tried to shut him up, but Henri was enjoying himself and paid no attention to them. He swung insolently around as Burt approached him. "You think you can beat me, do you?" Burt asked. He stood directly in front of Henri, his feet planted wide apart.

21

Henri slowly looked him up and down before smiling. "You would be the easiest of the three."

"You don't have the guts to back up your words, Bolkonsky," Burt said.

"You think not? Any time you say, Ferranto. I'll take on all three of you, one at a time. Just name the day and time."

"Okay. You've got a date Saturday at the gym at three."

"No holds barred?" Henri asked with one dark eyebrow raised.

"No holds barred." Burt grinned and nodded.

Vince was horrified. "Henri, are you insane? You can't take them on! You're neither a wrestler nor a boxer and you're still not in any condition to fight anyone much less those three!"

"Remember, Vance, this is a no holds barred fight. I don't have to be a wrestler nor a boxer to fight them. I may not win as easily as I said, but I will win."

Larry saw a strange light flickering in Henri's ice blue eyes and from past experience knew it boded no good for anyone.

The gym looked as if every man in the Academy had jammed into it. Henri walked through the room, his face a mask. The noisy crowd fell silent and parted for him, closing behind him as he passed through on his way to the ring in the center of the large room.

Some gave him an encouraging word or pat on the shoulder, others smiled silently, while others stared at him expecting him to go down in defeat, some shaking their heads at what they considered his folly.

Pete, Vance and Larry waited for him at the ring. John and Val appeared around the corner, joining the others as Henri walked up. Burt Ferranto had already stepped into the ring, warming up in his shorts and plimsols. Henri gave him an amused look; then slipped off his jacket and tie and rolled up his sleeves.

"Aren't you going to change?" Burt yelled down to him derisively as Henri changed his shoes. Steve and Mario came around the edge of the ring and eyed Henri with amusement.

Henri glanced up. "There is no need."

Vance caught Henri's arm as he was ready to swing over the ropes. "I know what you can do in a fight against uneven odds, Henri, but are you sure you want to go through with this?"

Henri smiled and swung himself up into the ring with the lithe coordinated grace of a young cheetah. The crown again fell silent in anticipation of the event unfolding before them.

One of the senior men arrived to stand as an unofficial referee, but Henri motioned him out of the ring. "This is a no holds barred fight. There will be no referee. The fight will be won when one of us yells quits or is knocked out. This was the agreement we made." Turning to Burt, he asked, "Do you still want to go on with it?"

Burt nodded, grinning and the would-be referee reluctantly climbed out of the ring.

"Don't you know that most of the men are betting on me? You'd better quite now, Bolkonsky, before I put you in the hospital." He planted his feet wide apart and placed his hands on his hips.

Henri's facial muscles formed a smile, but his eyes remained cold. Earlier he had told Vance, "I know I am no match for Burt if he can close in on me, but if I can keep him at a distance, I stand a good chance and I know how to do that."

Now, Burt said, "Okay. Ready?"

Henri nodded, stepped back and waited.

Burt circled while Henri pivoted watching him through narrowed eyes all the time a small smile playing about his lips. After a few minutes, Henri began to bait his opponent, his voice soft and deadly, "Come on, Burt. I'm no match for you. I'm wide open. What are you waiting for? You can't be afraid of me!" Circling away, he waited for Burt to make his first move.

Finally, Burt rushed him and Henri deftly sidestepped, bringing the edge of his right hand down across Burt's shoulder. Burt swung around and lunged for him, but Henri kept dancing out of his way, each time delivering a smashing blow of his own. He carefully calculated each one for its maximum punishing value, trying to wear Burt down to the point where Henri could close in on him. After a couple of minutes of playing cat and mouse with Burt, Henri became bored with the game and began to seriously close, quickly beating Burt to the floor. Contemptuously, he stepped back, looked down at Burt and walked away to the side of the ring.

Looking over the ropes, he called, softly, "Steven, it's your turn next. Let's see if you can do any better than your friend here."

Men jumped up onto the canvas and carried the unconscious Burt out of the ring and hurried toward the infirmary.

Henri turned his back to Steve and walked casually to the center of the ring. Snarling, Steve came over the ropes fast and rushed toward him, but being a boxer, pulled back to just out of arm's reach. He circled warily, looking for an opening. Henri continued to sidestep and dodge Steve's jabs and feints and waited patiently for his own openings. When he found them, he delivered his blows with lightening swiftness. It took no longer to wear Steve down than it had Burt, and Henri sent him to the floor with a final deadly jab.

Henri turned to the one he really wanted; the one who had been the instigator and leader of the trio. Mario looked into Henri's cold, hooded eyes and realized he had badly underestimated him. "I don't want to hurt you, Bolkonsky," he bluffed. "You've drawn your blood and proved your point. If you take me on, you will land in the hospital with the others."

Henri spread his hands on the ropes, stretched his arms out leaning on them, one shoulder slightly raised. "I suspected you were a coward, Mario, and now I know it. You don't have the guts to come up against me unless someone is holding my arms down for you." Soft and low, Henri's voice had a dangerous ring to it. Mario glared up at him from his spot beside the ring, his eyes full of anger. Before Mario saw him coming, Henri leaped over the ropes and in one fluid motion landed on top of him, sending him to the floor. "You are not going to be let off easily, Mario. Come on let's see if you can make your threat stick." Henri stood a little to one side of Mario as the man came painfully to his knees. Henri reached down, grabbed the front of Mario's shirt and dragged him to an upright position. With his open hand, he contemptuously slapped Mario's face twice then roughly pushed him away.

Mario looked around but saw no help. The crowd around the two had closed ranks. There was no escape. Henri again

24

stepped back, standing relaxed, waiting. As Mario turned toward him Henri said, "You've been watching me, Mario. You know how I fight, so you have an advantage over your friends. You're bigger than I and you outweigh me. You're a champion boxer and I don't know how to box. I've already fought two men. You are fresh. You have the advantage in every way except for that yellow streak down your back. You and your friends beat the bloody hell out of me a month ago when I couldn't defend myself. Now let's see if you can fight me when my arms are not held and you don't have your friends to help you." Henri's eyes held cold hard fury and his lips curled contemptuously. Slowly, he moved forward. His left fist shot out and connected solidly on Mario's jaw.

Mario circled away, unsuccessfully trying to sidestep Henri's blows. The men around them moved back giving the adversaries room. Henri struck every time he saw an opening, playing with Mario as he had with Burt and Steve; but now his blows were vicious, not meant just for punishment alone. Again and again, Henri beat Mario to his knees, each time dragging him back up onto his feet, deliberately delivering the most agonizing blows without letting him fall to the floor. Henri taking his now fully unlashed fury out on Mario continued to smash his fist into the face of the nearly unconscious man.

Vance knew that Henri would kill Mario if he were not stopped, stepped into the circle and grabbed Henri's arm as he was about to bring the edge of his hand down on Mario's neck. Henri dropped Mario, swinging to meet his new attacker. Standing over the unconscious body of his fallen foe, Henri's cold blue eyes met Vance's angry black ones.

"Why don't you take on someone your own size, Henri; someone who knows how to fight you and can use your same tactics? You've taken unfair advantage of these men to win your fight and prove your point. I was a commando too, remember. Come on Bolkonsky, let's see if you can beat me." Vance had moved out of Henri's reach and watched him carefully, knowing how deadly he could be.

Henri looked down at Mario, turned him over with his toe, then looked back at Vance. "All right. I've finished with him." The same cold smile played about his lips as it had done throughout his fight with the three men.

"In the ring, Bolkonsky," Vance said and climbed up over the ropes. He had seen the same blind fury in other men and knew Henri had to work it out of his system.

Henri climbed into the ring and the two men circled, watching each other intently. Evenly matched, both feinted, dodged and struck when an opening came; Henri with the lightening speed of a striking snake and Vance nearly as fast. Slowly, some of the fury began to ebb out of Henri's eyes and soon, he began to pull his punches. Now the men started to relax and spar with each other.

Finally, Henri stepped back, dropped his arms and said, "All right. Let's call it quits. You're good, but my argument is not with you. I'll concede this one."

"Okay by me," Vance said, smiling.

Henri leaped over the ropes; picked up his jacket and tie, turned and strode through the crowd looking neither to the right nor left, his face still a cold mask. The crowd again silently parted for him to pass through. He left the gym and moved across campus to his room. Changing into riding clothes, he pulled a long black cloak out of the footlocker, quickly went back down the stairs, picked up his weekend pass and hurried toward the stable. After saddling his horse, he headed into the hills to the café where the Russian Gypsies were playing.

Chapter Three

An old converted barn housed a café with small candlelit tables crowded close together to maximum capacity in the long rectangular room. A long old-fashioned Western bar ran the full length of the barn. Behind the bar, mirrors holding glass shelves filled with various shaped and shaded bottles, reflected the scene before them.   Red and white checkered tablecloths covered the tables near the entrance. These were reserved for patrons who wished to eat; the tables closer to the dance floor were bare, scarred and ringed by the hundreds of glasses placed on them over the years. For generations the cafe had been a favorite haunt of the Academy men as well as the local people, and the owner, Cory, knew nearly everyone by name.

"Mr. Cory, I'm becoming worried about the man at table seven." The young waiter stood anxiously at the owner's side.

Gory turned, glancing in the direction indicated. "Why?"

"Well, sir, he's drinking a bit heavily. He's gone through over half a bottle of Vodka in the past thirty minutes. Shall I stop serving him?"

"No. Not yet. He doesn't appear drunk and he has never gotten drunk in here before, nor has he ever caused any trouble."

"But, sir…"

"Keep serving him. He's a good customer, has been especially since the Gypsies arrived; besides, they'll look after him."

"He's not a Gypsy, is he sir?"

"No, but since the night he spoke to them in their own Romany, they've taken him into their family like a long lost brother and seem to look after him as their own."

"All right, sir, just as you say." The waiter sighed and hurried off to serve another customer.

Better keep a watchful eye on him even so, Cory thought. *There's an indefinable air of danger about him tonight and there may be trouble later.*

27

Henri sat sideways to his table beside the dance floor, his long legs stretched out in front of him, one hand playing with an empty shot glass, the other lying idly along his outstretched leg. He watched the Gypsy singers and dancers through narrowed eyes, a slight smile playing about his lips as he kept time to the music. His eyes sparkled dangerously as he watched one girl in particular. Black-haired with great dark eyes—the type seen in Egyptian wall paintings—she had the wild grace of a young leopard. The girl, Lita had been covertly watching Henri and had deliberately baited him several times during the evening as she whirled past his table. Now he waited.

Cory went to Pete, Vance, Larry and John as they stopped just inside the door and spoke in low tones. Larry nodded his head and the four men threaded their way to the table where Henri sat alone. He glanced briefly in their direction as they sat down, but went on watching the dancers without a word. The waiter returned to the table, poured more Vodka in his glass, took the others' orders, hesitated then left the bottle on the table. Henri raised the glass to his lips and drank it down in one gulp, never taking his eyes away from Lita.

Quietly, he shoved the bottle across the table, looking at his friends. "Ever tried this? It cures whatever ails you." His voice was low but something in his tone puzzled them. It held a hint of amusement, but also an arrogant dare. "Try some." It was obvious to Vance and the rest that the effect of the incident of that afternoon still had not worn off and Henri remained in a dangerous mood. It would be tempting fate to cross him right now.

A heavyset man, Liubov, the Primas of the Gypsies, wore his royal blue silk peasant blouse showing off his prosperous paunch to good advantage. When he smiled, his white teeth gleamed from behind a great bushy black beard. His black eyes danced and glowed. He too had been watching Henri; had also sensed the dangerous mood the young man was in; and he too worried. Liubov had noticed the attraction between Henri and Lita and felt, for Henri's sake, that he should encourage it. He knew a woman could take the fever out of a man's blood as nothing else. The first slow notes to the old Russian song "Dve Gitori" started as soon as the dancers stopped. Striding across the dance floor

Liubov bowed and in his booming bass voice asked Henri, "Boyar, will you do us the honor of singing with us again?" Imperceptibly, Henri nodded and rose with a lazy movement. With catlike grace, he strolled across the floor by the Gypsy's side.

The small band, which had been playing around the tune waiting to see what would happen, now burst forth and Henri's voice rose in a clear baritone. He sat on the edge of the dais clasping one knee in his hand, his eyes sparkling,

> "Dve gitari sa stenoyu
> Zhalabna zanyli
> Sertse pamyatny napyev
> Mily eta ty-li"

The Gypsies kept Henri singing for a long while, sometimes alone, sometimes in duet and sometimes in chorus. They sang many of the old Russian folk songs, as well as new, while part of the group danced or passed a bottle amongst themselves until Henri, laughingly, pleaded to dryness and the need for a rest and Vodka. Only then did they let him go.

As he sat at the table, his mood became more pensive than dangerous. The Gypsies danced again and again Henri watched, aware of the dark haired beauty's interest. Lita danced closer. She came toward him openly and provocatively, slipping into his lap. Putting one arm around her waist, he murmured, "Tvayi plyechaki" as he ran his fingers lightly up her back to her semi-bare shoulder.

Lita's lips nibbled at his ear then moved down toward his neck. Henri stretched his head sideways as a stallion does when a mare nips at him. A muscle in his jaw moved; his lips parted slightly; his nostrils flared taking in her scent. He breathed slowly and deeply; his eyes nearly slits. She gently nipped his neck and then a second time a little harder. Henri's head whirled toward her, his teeth just missing her lower cheek, as she pulled quickly away. With her forefinger, she traced the arch of his brow and the long lean line of his jaw. She smiled dreamily down at him as her fingers loosened his tie and unbuttoned his collar.

Henri relaxed against the back of the chair letting his fingers lightly trace the curve of her arm. She rose, caught his hand and pulled him to his feet, walking a little ahead of him as she led him to a side door and out of the café.

Gently, he put his arm around her waist and looked down at her, going unheedingly where she led. Presently, Lita stopped by her vardo parked under a tree by a little stream and stood looking full into his eyes. "Well, Gorgio Rai?" she asked in a low throaty voice, tempting him.

Henri pulled her to him and, crushing her mouth against his, lifted her in his arms. He carried her up the steps into the dark interior. As he laid her on the bed, his body arched over her, his hand brushed over her breasts, searching for the opening of her blouse, his body seeking hers. He had been without a woman for a long time and now he took her fiercely, the fire in him burning white-hot. There he spent the rest of the night reaching for her again and again but taking her more gently, softly.

"Henri, where the hell are you?"

The shout reached Henri's ears while he was still half asleep. Lita lay with a smile pulling up the corners of her mouth; her head on his shoulder; one arm languidly laying across his chest; long black hair flowing across the pillow.

Henri roused himself with an effort, gently placing a kiss on her forehead before rising to dress swiftly in the darkened interior. He appeared at the door of the vardo, his white shirt still partially unbuttoned. "Stop shouting, you will awaken the whole camp," he called softly, his cat-like eyes searching through the semi-darkness and white mist that shrouded the camp. "What do you want?"

"Thank God we found you." Vance appeared out of the mist around the corner of the caravan with Larry close on his heels. "The general just got back from Edinburgh and wants to see you. Hurry, he looks like Vesuvius about to erupt." The two men stood at the foot of the steps looking up at Henri.

Henri's blue eyes, which had held a sleepy look, now sharpened. He withdrew into the caravan, reappearing in a few minutes fully dressed and ready. He dropped from the platform and went around back to saddle his horse. "We'll drive you down and you can fetch your horse later," Larry said.

"No. I would rather ride. I know of a shortcut and will get there as fast as by the road." Something in his manner brooked no argument. Vance shrugged his shoulders and climbed into their jeep.

Henri swung into the saddle, about to ride away, when Lita came out onto the steps of the vardo, a brightly colored housecoat clutched about her. "Gorgios Rai," she called softly, "Are you going without saying goodbye?"

Henri turned his horse's head and rode up beside her. Leaning down from his saddle, he kissed her gently. "Goodbye, *sundarinya*, perhaps we will meet again someday."

"*Ja develesa.*" Lita stood with sadness in her eyes as he set his horse into a canter and disappeared into the woods.

Most of the Academy men had finished breakfast and were strolling in small-scattered groups around the parade ground. Riding through them, Henri was aware of eyes covertly watching him and guessed at the rumors which must have run through the Academy as soon as General Dayton returned. He gave no indication of his awareness, deliberately masking his thoughts behind a cold indifferent face, his head held rigidly straight, looking neither to the right nor left.

General Dayton, about to enter his house, paused at the door to wait until Henri dismounted and came up the stairs. "You wanted to see me, sir?" Henri saluted.

"Yes, come inside. General Dayton turned on his heel, leading the way. Henri undid the clasp of his cloak, throwing it over his arm as he followed.

Inside his office, the general snapped, "Shut the door Mr. Bolkonsky." He sat behind his desk eyeing Henri coldly for a full minute. "Will you kindly give me an explanation of yesterday afternoon's episode? You put three men into the hospital, all of them with broken bones and one with a possible concussion."

"Henri stood at rigid attention looking at a spot just above the general's stern angry eyes. "Yes, sir." He kept his voice devoid of any expression. "Those three men beat me up a month ago. Yesterday, I returned the compliment."

"I see." Anger remained in the General's eyes. "Did you know who they were at that time?"

"Yes, sir, I did."

"Are they the same men with whom you had trouble before?"

"Yes, sir."

"Then why the devil did you not say so at the time?" General Dayton snapped.

"I preferred to deal with them myself, sir, in my own way."

"I see." General Dayton drummed his fingers on the top of his desk. "All right, Mr. Bolkonsky, you will not be dismissed from the Academy this time, but remember there is no room here for personal revenge. If at anytime in the future this sort of thing happens again and you know the names of the culprits, you are to report it immediately. You are not to take any action on your own again. Is that clear?"

"Yes, sir."

"You will be confined to the Academy for the next month. There are to be no more weekend passes until that time."

"Yes, sir."

"You are dismissed."

When Henri hesitated, General Dayton raised an angry eyebrow.

"Permission to speak, sir."

"Granted." The general's voice remained gruff.

"What's going to happen to those three, sir?"

"I haven't decided yet, very probably, they will be dismissed.

Henri knew he was courting an explosion, but went on, forcing his voice to remain calm, "I hope you do not decide to dismiss them, sir; it would be a waste of three good lives and potentially excellent officers."

General Dayton leaned back in his chair, a frown creasing his forehead. "Stand at ease, Mr. Bolkonsky. Now just what are you trying to say?"

Henri's expression hadn't changed from its respectful mask, but his voice took on a new intensity. "I'm trying to say that I do not think they should be dismissed from the Academy, sir."

"And why not?"

I've learned something about them from the other men here. Their records have been spotless up until now. Leonardo and Velp are on the Honour Roll and Ferranto most probably will be within the next month. Two of them have said they were considering making the army their career. If they are dismissed now, their lives would be forever marked and any career in the army might as well be washed off and forgotten. They would have to explain their dismissal from the Academy on any application in the business world. It simply wouldn't be fair."

"Sit down, Mr. Bolkonsky. Just exactly why are you, of all people, pleading their case? They put you in the hospital badly beaten and yet you tell me I should not dismiss them for such actions? I'm afraid I don't understand you. What exactly is your reasoning?"

Henri sighed with relief, realizing he would receive a fair hearing. "Sir, it's true that they beat me into a bloody pulp, but on the other side of the coin, I did the same to them. If you cashier them, in all fairness and justice, you would have to do the same to me. My crime is the same as theirs with one difference; that difference being that it was cold-blooded revenge on my part, while there were extenuating circumstances in their case."

"Go on, Bolkonsky."

"I am in a privileged position here; they are not. Two of them will probably be career men; I will not. I am here for a specific purpose of security, when summer comes, I will leave and not return, so if I am cashiered it will not really matter. When all this is over, I am going into a business that my uncle owns and I will not need to look for a job. But for them it means their lives.

"My final reason is that they have had enough punishment already, openly and in front of the whole Academy. I think they have learned a lesson they may never have learned and will be better men and officers because of it."

The general had listened quietly throughout and now asked, "You speak of extenuating circumstances. What exactly do you mean by that?"

"Sir, in the United States, as far as most people were concerned, only national armies fought the war: American, British,

Russian all against the Nazis. They never or rarely heard about the fifth one, the resistance groups and even less about the Intelligence men who worked behind the lines. Leonardo, Ferranto and Velp all lost family members in the war. Leonardo lost a brother who was viciously beaten to death by the S.S. in a detention camp; Ferranto lost a brother who was captured and shot after his plane crashed; and Velp lost his father during the Normandy landings.

"I am twenty-seven years old and lived in Europe during the war. I did not belong to any of the armies. The men here didn't know that I was an undercover intelligence agent. One of them found an old German newspaper clipping with my picture in a Nazi uniform. The article stated that I had been decorated with the Iron Cross by Hitler. Also I had been appointed an Aide to General von Graf. This is all true. The name in the article was different, but the picture was unmistakable.

"That coupled with the fact that I have chewed all three of them out several times, most recently for carelessly handling their rifles." General Dayton again raised an eyebrow and Henri digressed. "They had been playing around with a rifle and it went off narrowly missing one of the men standing in a group with me. I read them out in front of everyone and spoke in German, or rather, swore in German. This hurt their pride. They couldn't get back at me right then since the instructor was standing nearby and made no attempt to stop or reprimand me. I must admit, I was rather overbearing at the time and they had a right to be angry. I certainly would have been!"

"I see. Go on."

"As you know, sir, the desire for revenge is a deep seated part of human nature. The desire to strike back when you have been hit or someone you love has been murdered is natural. They didn't have an opportunity to go overseas and fight and, thinking I had been a Nazi, I was the closest person they could lay their hands on. I know that desire for revenge for I have felt it many times. My family was murdered at Dachau but I was able to legitimately take my revenge during the war. Yesterday was another typical example of the same thing." Henri paused, glancing at the general. "Am I making sense to you, sir?"

"Yes, Mr. Bolkonsky, I think you are."

"Then I ask you please not to cashier them, sir."

"I will certainly take your words into account when I make my decision, Mr. Bolkonsky. You may go now and thank you for your frankness with me."

"Thank you, sir." Henri rose, saluted, bowed and left the room.

General Dayton sat at his desk, a thoughtful look in his eyes. He'd come across men like Bolkonsky before who meted out their own justice when it came to personal matters or their pride. They often had proven to be the best fighters, and leaders with guts and initiative, perfect material for the type of work that Bolkonsky did during the war, but he'd never found one who would turn around and defend his enemies' actions. Dayton sighed and pulled three folders toward him to study before making his final decision on the fates of the men, but he already knew what that decision would be.

Chapter Four

Henri sat behind the desk quietly surveying the faces of the eight men sitting in a rough semi-circle around him. Lying on the desk in front of him was the German article which had caused so much trouble. "Today we will not talk about the assignment," he began. "I believe an explanation is long overdue and it is about time some misconceptions and misinterpretations were cleared up. I would like to talk about this article in particular and other things in general."

He leaned back in his chair, his eyes riveted somewhere in the middle ground between himself and the men. "The story behind this article really starts in 1933 when my father took the post of Professor of Political Science at the University of Berlin. At that time, Hitler was just coming into power and, because of the depression in Germany amongst other factors, people of all classes flocked to the Nazi party. My father was against Fascism, Communism or any form of dictatorship and in his classes, preached against the ideologies Hitler and his group were advocating. Finally, in early 1938, my father was dismissed from his post at the University and placed under house arrest by the Gestapo. He had been warned many times to conform to the Nazi line, but had refused to do so. The Nazis had tried to get him to join the party. Himmler even went to the extent of making him an honorary officer in the S.S. Father promptly refused the "honor." It was shortly after this that he was dismissed.

"A few weeks later the Gestapo came to the house late one night and arrested my father. We had no idea where he was. My mother called everyone who might have a clue to where he had been taken. She even went to Gestapo headquarters in Berlin but to no avail. He had simply disappeared like so many others. About a week later, the Gestapo came again and arrested the entire family. All of us were taken to their Headquarters. All, that is, except my little sister, Maria, who was three months old at the time. The next evening, we were all shipped to Dachau and questioned separately." Henri's lips pulled back in a sardonic smile. "None too gently, I might add. Afterward, we were taken to the basement of one of the buildings and there we saw my father again.

Henri rose and walked around the desk. Half sitting on its edge with the heels of his palms resting on its top, he continued, "I will not go into details, but everyone of my family were murdered there in front of my eyes. Why I was not, remains a mystery, but I'm sure they had their reasons. They do nothing without a reason.

"I was placed in one of the barracks with other prisoners. A week later, I managed to escape and make my way back to Berlin where I found my baby sister and our servant, Igor, still in the house. We made our way across Germany with help from friends of my father, thence to England. I sent Marie and Igor to my uncle in the States and I went to live with a distant cousin in the South of France.

"There I formed a small group of friends who would join me in a resistance group when the war came. We all felt it would come eventually and began to prepare for it. The Germans walked into France in 1940 and my friends and I went underground. Not too long afterward the British Secret Intelligence Service contacted me. M16, as SIS was known during the war, had heard about me and my group through my Godfather. They asked me to come over to England, which I did. I insisted on having commando training before going to work for them.

"I came to the British Commando School at Auchnacarry near this Academy. When I finished the course, I returned to London. I took a basic course in intelligence work, returned to the Continent and to my group where I trained them in what I had learned in England.

"After going on a few commando raids, I was assigned to act as liaison between various underground groups throughout Europe. With my perfect German, I was made a Wehrmacht officer, a lieutenant, because I would attract the least attention that way and could travel freely through Europe.

37

"The Bolkonsky's have intermarried with many of the aristocratic houses of Europe, amongst them the German von Spieldau family. Since I could indirectly legitimately hold the title, I appropriated the name and Germanized Henri to Heinrich. The von Spieldau line died out a generation ago, so I was safe using the name. M16 needed to make contact with the resistance groups in Hungary, Poland and Russia, so I was given forged papers sending me to the Russian front.

"In one of those battles during the winter, I was wounded and sent back to Germany. At that time, Dr. Goebbles needed something good to say for his propaganda machine and by pure chance he picked me and arranged for me to receive the Iron Cross from Hitler at Berchtesgarten. Then he had me appointed Aide to General von Graf and raised to the rank of Captain. M16 was extremely pleased to hear of this. It put me in an excellent position to gather intelligence almost from the source; however, the S.S. knew highly secret information was being leaked to the Allies and they knew it had to be coming from a high place.

"Things became sticky, but it was not until almost the end of the war that they actually caught up with me. Fortunately, I managed to escape across the lines and was eventually sent back to London.

"That is the story behind the article and what and who I was during the war. A lot of what I say cannot be verified, but some of the early days of my career as a commando, can be substantiated by several men here at the Academy." Henri paused. "Now, gentlemen, are there any questions?"

Silence greeted him as the men stirred uneasily. Finally, Mario asked, "Why was your father not arrested earlier, say in 1934 or 1935?"

"He was a very influential man with close friends in high places, amongst them some of the German aristocracy to whom we were related and who were on the General Staff. He was also close friends of the British and American Ambassadors and to some of the English aristocracy. Hitler did not want to stir up British anger over anything at that time. I think he hoped to make the British his allies or, short of that, keep them neutral until he felt strong enough to declare war."

"I didn't know that Dachau or any other concentration camps existed as early as 1938," said Burt.

"Yes, it had been in existence since 1933, shortly after Himmler was appointed Police Commissioner of Munich. At first, it was mainly a camp where Himmler held arrested Communists, Social Democrats and other 'undesirables.'"

"Were you in on the July 20th plot to assassinate Hitler?"

"No, although I did know about it. Some good friends of mine were in on it and lost their lives as a result. I came under suspicion, but was never arrested."

Just then, the bell rang signaling the end of the class. Henri moved around the desk to his chair. "Any more questions, gentlemen?" He scanned the faces in front of him. "No? Right. We will meet again at the usual time on Thursday. You know the assignment."

Mario, Steve and Burt stopped at Henri's desk. Mario spoke for the three of them, "My. Bolkonsky, I think the three of us owe you an apology for what has happened. Also thanks for going to bat for us with General Dayton."

Henri glanced up from the article which still lay in front of him. A fleeting smile touched his lips. He nodded. "No thanks necessary. I'll see you on Thursday.

Chapter Five

Winter roared onto the campus. Henri and Vance quickened their stride over the rippled powdered snow with each blast of wind that swept across the river and the moors. Clouds scudded across the sky in large dark masses while a water haloed moon rode full, intermittently bathing the Academy with its pale light. The ancient knurled trees cast their shadows on the snow-covered ground and waved cold bare branches in the icy wind. The old, grey stone buildings stood black and solid in the night, showing yellow frosted eyes to those passing by.

"I hope the O.D. has some hot coffee in his office," Vance shouted into Henri's ear. Henri grinned behind the heavy wool scarf wrapped around his face. They both had turned their collars up around their ears so only their eyes showed. "I'm sure looking forward to a hot shower and warm bed. God! I'm nearly frozen!" Vance yelled.

Both men staggered, as a new blast hit them. Leaning against the wind, they shivered deeper into their coats as they left the trees surrounding the quad and parade ground. Crossing the road, they were within a few feet of the stairs to their dormitory when a bullet ricocheted off the corner of the building close to Henri's head. They instinctively hit the ground together, rolling to cover in the shadows as another bullet hit the edge of the building.

Crouching against the wall, Henri swept his eyes over the campus. At the same time, they both spotted a shadow of movement amongst the trees they had just left. "Stay here and keep an eye on him," Henri whispered. "I'm going to try to circle around behind him." Vance nodded, as Henri silently slipped off along the wall of the building.

It seemed like a long time before Vance saw Henri dart across the road to reach the shelter of trees far down and out of sight of their hunter.

Three other pairs of eyes watched the deadly drama playing out. Mario had been standing by the window of his room when he saw Henri and Vance suddenly drop to the ground and roll out of sight. He called Steve and Burt over to see what was happening and they had a bird's eye view of the deadly black and white shadow play.

By now, Henri was within a few yards of the shooter when he moved, starting toward the spot where Vance and Henri had been when the shots were fired. Henri froze, pressing himself against the bole of a tree. He watched his man carefully work his way forward. Suddenly, the man swerved, backtracking in the direction of the tree behind which Henri stood. Vance picked up a stone and threw it in a different direction. The man whirled searching for the source of the noise. Henri slipped from his hiding place. Moving noiselessly up behind his quarry, he gave one quick chop across the side of the man's neck.

Vance ran up as Henri leaned down to pick up the rifle. "Do you have any idea who he is, Henri?"

"Not the foggiest, but we'll soon find out when he comes around. Go call Jim Stevens at this number." He handed Vance a piece of paper. "Tell him to get over here fast."

Henri stepped back and, snow still swirling around him, leaned against a tree, the rifle nestled in the crook of his arm, ready to be brought into instant action, if necessary. His prisoner groaned and tried to sit up. "All right get on your feet, mister. Keep your hands above your head and walk toward that building on your right," he snapped.

He marched his assailant into the O.D.'s office as Mario, Steve and Burt came bounding down the stairs. "Now, face the wall and lean your hands against it."

"This man was using Vance and me for target practice," Henri said, handing the rifle to the startled O.D.

Henri quickly and expertly frisked the man, pulling out a billfold and a small black book. Sitting casually on the edge of the desk, he went through the billfold, taking out two pieces of paper.

"All right, you may sit on that chair in the corner." Henri studied his prisoner with cold eyes for a few minutes before asking, "Is Paul Weaver your real name?"

A small muscle twitched spasmodically in the man's cheek, but his thin straight mouth remained clamped shut. He dropped his eyes to the floor and maintained stony silence. Henri reached over taking the rifle from Val, quietly slipping off the safety catch. "I do not want to have to ask the question again – sir." Still, Weaver did not answer.

Henri raised the rifle, pointed it a fraction of an inch to one side of Weaver's head and squeezed the trigger. The bullet crashed into the wall. "What the…" The O.D. started to rise, but a warning glance from the grim faces of the former commandos in the group froze him in mid-air. The noise of the shot brought other men on the run, but Larry and John prevented them from entering.

"Yes," The fear, which had lurked behind Weaver's eyes, now leaped to the fore, draining his face of what little color had been there.

"So, you do have a voice." A small sarcastic smile slipped across Henri's face. "Who gave you the order to come here?"

Again Weaver closed his mouth until Henri slid another cartridge into the chamber, pointing the rifle at him. "A man called Hans."

"What is his last name?"

"I don't know."

"Where does he live?"

"I don't know."

"How do you get your orders?"

"Weaver hesitated for a fraction of a second before answering. "Over the telephone." His eyes slid toward the black book lying on the table. He quickly looked away, but not soon enough.

Smiling, Henri flipped the book open and removed two loose sheets of paper. "Careless of you, was it not?" He snapped the book closed. "You are lying my friend. What is Hans' last name?"

"I tell you I don't know!"

Henri walked over to him, pulled him up with one hand and chopped him first in the midriff; twice more just over the kidneys. Holding the man up by his shirtfront, Henri said in a low voice, "Now what is Hans' last name?"

"Coleman," Weaver gasped.

Mario and Steve started to move forward. "Keep out of it," Larry said.

Henri shoved Weaver back into his seat. "Now, where does Hans Coleman live?"

"In Edinburgh."

"That's better. What is his address?"

"I don't know."

"My friend, I do not want to have to hurt you again." The soft words belied the cold hardness in Henri's eyes. "Again, what is Hans Coleman's address?"

Weaver hunched over, his arms crossed, his body shaking. "I tell you, I don't know! I get my orders by telephone or in a letter drop. That's the truth!"

Henri regarded him through narrowed eyes, "All right. Where is the letter drop?"

"It's a loose brick under the rear staircase of a building on High Street."

"What is the address of the building?"

Before Weaver could respond, Jim and three Constables walked into the room. Taking in the scene, Jim strode over to Henri. Henri picked up the rifle and handed it to him, "What happened here?"

Henri told him the events of the evening and gave him the code book and the two sheets of paper containing messages. Jim nodded and glanced at the bullet hole in the wall. "Did you rough him up?"

"A little." Henri shrugged. "it didn't take much to loosen his tongue. If he is representative of the Nazis in this country, then I have nothing to fear."

Jim's eyes blazed. "If this ever happens again and you catch the man, don't ever repeat this kind of performance. Remember, this is Scotland, not the Continent, and this is not war time." Henri

43

raised an eyebrow, a cold light dancing in his eyes. With a curt nod, Jim left to catch up with the Constables and their prisoner.

"Okay, Henri, what is this all about," Vance asked.

"I am due to testify at the Nuremberg trials this summer and the Nazis want to stop me. That's all."

"What do you mean the Nazis want to stop you?" Mario shouted. "The war is over." They were beaten and their top men are either captured or killed!"

Henri smiled a curious sad smile, "You really believe that? I'm sorry to disillusion you, but just because the main Nazi leaders have been hanged or committed suicide does not mean the party no longer exists. Many Nazis remain in Europe and in South America, lying low waiting for the day they can restart their operations. The three to be hanged this summer for murdering my family are three of their key people."

"So that's why you're here. You're in hiding," Vance cut in.

"Right, old man. The best protective coloring is a uniform; everyone looks the same. Short of putting me in solitary confinement, they pulled strings and registered me at this Academy. I could have stayed at home, but that would have put what is left of my family in greater danger; so to draw the fire away from them, I came here. Now my cover has apparently been blown, but it is still the safest place for me at the moment."

"Bloody hell!" Val said in sudden realization, "That's what that nonsensical conversation was all about. Damn! I'm slow on the up-take these days."

Henri's grin turned to laughter. Grimly, the four former commandos nodded and without a word decided that at least two of them would stick close to Henri until it was time for him to leave for Europe.

"Has your family arrived yet, Henri?" Val dropped into a chair by the fire n the recreation room and stretched luxuriously.

"Um hum." Henri glanced up from the book he was reading. "They came yesterday."

"Where are they staying? Which hotel?"

"None. My uncle decided it would be more fun to camp, so they are over by the edge of the Loch."

"Camp? In this weather?" They must be mad!" Vance settled cross-legged on the floor in front of the fire.

Henri laughed. "The brought up the yurt."

"Val and Vance looked at each other saying in unison, "The yurt? What's that?"

Henri cocked his head to one side, an amused smile playing about his mouth. "It's a large round tent made of animal hides or heavy felt. It was used by the Mongols, easy to put up and take down. It still is used by some nomadic tribes. For some reason known only to her, one of my aunts brought one out of Russia when they escaped—maybe with the idea of living in it in exile in the west—so now we use it when we camp."

"Mad!" Val said. "I told you they are all mad—these Russians."

"I'm sure glad these exercises have finished," Larry commented to no one in particular as he joined the group. "These last three days have been exhausting and I'm looking forward to this family weekend."

"You're out of training and becoming lazy in your old age." Henri grinned.

"It will be nice to relax. Have you got a girl for the dance tomorrow?" Val asked Henri.

"Um. My cousin Carlotta." Henri's face became a blank, but a devil danced in his eyes. "I rather hesitate to ask, but I wonder…um…well…would all of you do me a great favor?"

"Sure," Val answered for them all.

"Promise to have at least one dance with her. You see Carlotta is…ah…well…a very nice girl, but…how can I put it…a little plump. She isn't terrible attractive…on the plain side really…and a bit clumsy. I do want her to have a good time and it would not look terribly good if I danced with her all evening, so I would appreciate it if you each would take her around the floor at least once." Henri had trouble controlling his face as he pictured his cousin who could turn the head of any man she met; whose blond beauty had every man behaving like a doormat for her exclusive use; whose delicate frame was a willowy seven and a half stone; and who moved with a ballerina's grace.

"Okay, sure." Vance looked disappointed at Henri's description. "By the way, who else of your family are up here?"

"My aunt and uncle, my two cousins, Alexei and Jean, and my sister, Maria. Philippe could not come as he is down with a bad cold." Henri hid a yawn with the back of his hand. "I think I'll go up to bed early tonight."

"Who is accusing whom of becoming lazy in his old age?" Larry laughed.

"Well, we do have the full dress parade in the morning and the demonstrations in the afternoon." Val grinned. "Think I'll join you Henri."

Before they could leave, one of the men barked, "Attention!" General Dayton walked into the room. He swept his eyes over the assembled group. "Do any of you know where Pete McGovern, Mario Leonard and Burt Ferranto are?" His parade voice boomed loud in the now quiet room.

"McGovern was to do a rock climb as part of his exercise, sir," Henri said.

"What about Ferranto and Leonardo?"

"I believe they were to go with him, sir. I wasn't here when they left, but perhaps their roommate might know which of the climbs they used."

General Dayton turned to his aid, "Get him immediately."

When Steve Velp arrived, the general asked him the same question, but Velp's answer was no more helpful that Henri's had been. "They went rock climbing, sir."

"Where?"

"They said they had a choice of either Old Baldy or the Eagle's Nest, sir, but I don't know which one they chose."

"I want everyone assembled and ready to move out in half an hour," Dayton commanded, turned on his heel and left the room.

"They should have been back by now," Henri said to Velp. "Which is the most difficult to climb?"

"The Eagle's Nest."

"Then that's the one they probably climbed."

"Yeah, and with the weather closing in like it is, we're going to have a hell of a time locating them."

The men were already formed into companies in front of their buildings on the snow packed parade ground by the time General Dayton drove up. Trucks parked along the road held tents and equipment ready to move out. Their drivers stamped their feet and blew on their gloved hands to keep warm. Floodlights lit up the assembled men dressed in their heavy grey greatcoats ready to climb into the waiting trucks.

General Dayton watched as the last of the men formed up on the double. He signaled Henri out of his group. "You are assigned to the lead jeep with Mr. Forrest. Ferranto and Leonardo's fathers will go with you. You are to head for the Eagle's Nest and search for the three missing men."

"Move out!" the words blasted up and down the line.

The roar of trucks revving up split the still night air. Vance greeted Henri, introduced him to the others and handed him a pair of field glasses. Vance put the vehicle in gear and drove out the gates, General Dayton, Dr. White, Mr. McGovern and, unknown to Henri, Pete's brother, Dave followed in the two cars directly behind them.

They drove most of the way through the white countryside in silence, each man sunk in his own thoughts and worries. At a little after dawn, they caught their first glimpse of the Eagle's Nest.

"Pull over here for a minute, Vance," Henry said. "I want to get a better look at it from this angle."

The great scarred and serrated rock, bathed in light from the rising sun, thrust its jagged black head defiantly into the clear pale sky like some prehistoric tyrannosaurus. Raising his field glasses, Henri went over its face centimeter by centimeter, pinpointing what could be ledges, but also could be merely shadows. Turning away, he came face to face with Mario's father.

"Did you see anything?" Leonardo's voice grated in the stillness.

"No, sir. We're too far away." Henri replied. "Vance. drive up the road a couple of miles. We'll scan the face again from there." Henri settled back in his seat and watched the rock face as it appeared and disappeared through the trees. He felt hostility emanating from Mr. Leonardo, and sensed that Mario's father

47

thought he was stalling. He could also feel Ferranto's eyes on him and wondered what was in his thoughts.

No more disparate group of men could have been brought together than the three fathers. When their sons were discovered missing, they had been called to the Academy from nearby Fort William where they were staying for family weekend.

Renaldo Leonardo, a tall imposing man wore his iron grey hair longer than the current style. Deep-set grey eyes glittered under heavy dark eyebrows. His mouth, which could smile easily, sat slim and straight beneath his slightly bridged nose. A long face with long prominent cheekbones, slim hands with manicured finger nails, and expensively tailored clothes completed the picture. Henri guessed he was originally from Northern Italy— Venice or Milan.

The other two men were almost his exact antithesis. The short Ferranto appeared to have been squeezed into his clothes and in the light his thick black curly hair shone almost blue above brown eyes set wide in a square face. Sardinian or Sicilian, Henri thought.

McGovern, the classic Texan—tall, rangy, rawboned—had the same red hair as his son. Deeply tanned, his blue eyes held a perpetual squint, small crows' feet radiating from their corners. Craggy, rough hewn, but full of warmth and friendliness, he looked as if he would be more at home on a horse than riding through the snow in a jeep. Henri took an instant liking to this quiet man.

Vance stopped the jeep on the lip of a small concave valley while Henri climbed out again. Now, He could see an area of the Nest that obviously was a slide area. His heart sank at the sight. Examining the evilly rugged face again, he stopped…riveting on one particular spot. He swung the glasses away, then moved them back again to make sure it wasn't a trick of light. Standing beside him, General Dayton asked, "What do you see, Bolkonsky?"

"Look about halfway up, sir, just to the left of that hump; you'll see a ledge. I think someone is on it; although I can't be sure."

General Dayton moved his glasses to where Henri directed and stared at the spot for a long time, "Um, you may be right."

48

"Now, if you go straight up and a little to the right, I think there's another ledge with another person. I haven't located the third man yet."

Dayton nodded his head. "Okay. Let's go."

Henri returned to the jeep. "Could you see who the people on the ledges were? Let me have the glasses," Leonardo demanded.

"We are too far away to make an identification, sir. I doubt very much that we will know until we get to the ledge itself."

Vance turned off the road, driving down a dirt track leading directly to the foot of the rock face. Bumping over the rough ground of the valley floor, he pulled over and turned off the ignition. Men, trucks and jeeps spread out over the valley. The jeep and the two cars had stopped on a level area somewhat higher than the rest of the valley. They were protected from the wind by a semicircle of trees. The radio and medical tents were already being put up and men were busy setting up General Dayton's quarters, as well as those for the parents. Dayton, the doctor and several others consulted near the radio tent while loudspeakers were placed in strategic places.

"Is there anyone here with rescue experience on a cliff like that?" Henri heard General Dayton ask.

"Not that I know of." Colonel Grey had joined the group around the general only moments before.

"Ask over the loudspeakers," Dayton ordered.

When no one responded, Henri and the commandos stepped forward but Dayton ignored them and snapped, "Radio out and find the nearest rescue group and get them here."

Henri stood next to the radio tent studying the sky when the message came in that the nearest group was in Wales and it would take thirty-six hours to get to this remote area of Scotland. The general paced impatiently up and down in front of the tent. Those around him could almost see him thinking. Henri knew that what it came down to for the general was whether to send the commandos to attempt a rescue or to wait for the team from Wales. The real problem was that no one knew if the men on the mountain were hurt

49

or, if so, how badly. If they weren't already dead, a thirty-six hour wait could seal their fate.

Henri broke into the Dayton's thoughts. "I think I can get them down, sir. That face is not too hard for an experienced rock man."

Dr. White broke in quickly, "I absolutely refuse to let you go up there, Bolkonsky. It's out of the question."

"I have a good chance of getting them down."

"You have an even better chance of killing yourself! We will wait for the rescue group."

"You don't have time to wait," Henri snapped. "Do you see those storm clouds banking up on the horizon? By this evening you will have a first class storm and those men up there don't stand a chance of surviving it."

"Exactly how much experience do you have, Mr. Bolkonsky?" General Dayton asked.

"I was with a mountain rescue team in the Alps, as well as rock climbing with my father every spring and fall, sir. I also had to lead commando groups up faces similar to this one during the war. I know I can get them down and time is running out."

"Mr. Bolkonsky is still recovering and in no condition to do rescue work of this kind, General," the doctor said.

"That face is not as difficult as it looks to an amateur's eyes," Henri cut in. "At least let me try, sir. The men don't stand a chance of lasting until the Welsh team gets here.

"We have four other former commandos here," Dayton said. "They can go up with you, as well as any of the others who have done some training in rock climbing."

"Give me just one of the commandos, sir. I'm acquainted with their skills and this climb is more than any of them has attempted before."

"All right, get moving, Bolkonsky, but if you feel you cannot make it and come down alive, you are to quit! Take a commando with you and the other three will stand by in case of trouble."

Henri turned to the four commandos. "Vance, you've had some experience in mountain rescue work, want to join me?"

"You bet!"

"Do you have any morphine?" Henri asked Dr. White. "And give us some sterile needles, bandages, splints and anything else you think we may need."

Reluctantly, the doctor turned to get a pack ready for the climb. Henri, Vance and Colonel Grey moved off to secure the needed climbing gear.

Henri spoke with Colonel Grey in terse sentences as he carefully checked the assembled equipment. Dave McGovern, standing quietly in the background, smiled to himself as he watched Henri's swift deft movements and his complete concentration on the job at hand. The low voice, quiet, yet in full command, took Dave back to a dim room hidden under a barn floor where Henri quietly and efficiently attended wounded crew members by candlelight. The same serious look on his face; the same deft movements; the same complete concentration he had then as now.

Dave's memory flashed back to their first meeting. Dave was in England when the war broke out, a member of the RAF and a bomber co-pilot. One night, on a mission near Dunkirk, flak raced at them from every direction. They were hit hard. The pilot spotted an open field and brought the crippled plane down. It was a hell of a rough landing and flames burst out in the tail section. The pilot was shot up badly and Dave, pinned in his seat, his left leg crushed beneath him, thought he had bought it, until suddenly Henri and one of his men, Etienne, burst into the cockpit. Working feverishly they got the old man free and Etienne dragged him out of the plane, while Henri turned to Dave. "Hang on, we'll get you out of here." Pulling at twisted metal until his hands bled, Henri pulled Dave from his seat and carried him out. The two of them had not gone far when the whole show went up. Henri threw Dave to the ground and covered him with his own body to protect him from flying shrapnel

Later, Dave learned from Etienne that Henri and his men had gotten the whole crew out. Dave had been the last one. Etienne also told him that Henri had ordered all of his men to stay clear of the plane because he knew it would blow any minute, but still Henri had stayed to bring him out.

Henri and his small group hid the bomber crew, nursed them until they could be moved, then escorted them to the Channel and sent them back to England. Etienne told him that their group often watched during raids for ditched planes and that they had become quite expert in rescuing crews from under the noses of the Nazis.

Dave's thoughts were broken when Dr. White arrived handing Henri the supplies he had requested. "Be careful, Bolkonsky. You are not yet up to par and that leg can still go out on you."

"Stop worrying about me. I'll be fine." Henri grinned. "I have a lot of reserves I can call upon when needed. I'll get down all right." He hoisted his pack, picked up the ropes and started to leave with Vance.

"I've sent a man from the Academy to where your family is camped and they'll be guided here immediately. Be careful, Bolkonsky. We don't want to lose you or Forrest. Good luck!"

"Thanks. By the way, it would be a good idea to keep everyone away from the base of the cliff. I see signs of rock slides." He started to leave, but turned back, "Uncle Paul and Alexei are highly experienced mountain climbers. If things become sticky, I'll signal and they can come up to help."

"Why the hell didn't you say so earlier. We could wait for them to arrive."

"We don't have time, sir." Henri glanced at the sky. "It will take at least two hours for them to arrive and that storm is coming in too rapidly."

Dayton looked at the sky and nodded, "Okay. Carry on." He watched Henri and Vance stride off with a quiet thoughtful look in his eyes. The men stood in a small silent group before the tents, each now pinning their hopes on two young men who very well might not make it off the cliff alive themselves. Let alone be able to rescue the three men already up there.

Chapter 6

Henri and Vance reconnoitered the base of the cliff, but could not find the original starting point the three men had used. It took them nearly three hours to inch their way up the cliff using every crevice and protruding knob of rock. It was a slow laborious climb, much harder than Henri expected. They found few ledges or places where they could stop to rest and Henri's arms and legs ached from the unaccustomed strain. The sun blazed and Henri paused frequently to wipe the perspiration from his face.

Both breathing rapidly, they finally reached the first narrow ledge. "Oh my God! Who is it?" Vance cried.

Henri barely had enough room to straddle the body lying across the ledge. Carefully, He turned over the limp unresisting form. "It's Pete."

Henri checked Pete's pulse and ran his hands over his body feeling for broken bones. Pete groaned and opened his eyes. "Glad to see you awake, old man."

"Where did you come from?" Pete asked when he was able to focus on the hazy faces hanging in the air above him. "What are you doing here?"

"Oh, Vance and I thought we'd take a little stroll and popped round to see how you were doing." Henri quipped. "Are you in any pain?"

Pete tried to match Henri's light-hearted manner and attempted a weak smile. "Yeah, but not much at the moment. It's only bad when I try to move. I think my right leg is broken; I can't move it."

Henri bent down and with gentle probing fingers checked the leg. Pete's body arched as Henri carefully began to splint it. "Steady, Pete. I'll try not to hurt you, but I'm going to have to splint it. If the pain gets bad, I have some morphine I can give you."

"Yah," Pete grunted. "Only take it easy will you? Have you found Mario and Burt?"

"Not yet." Henri worked quickly and deftly. "From the ground, I spotted someone on a ledge a little above you, but I can't seem to find anyone else."

"That would be Burt. He was the second man on the rope. Mario should be somewhere in between us—over to our left."

"Okay. We'll go up, get Burt and maybe we can spot Mario from there. There, your leg is splinted. We're going to put you on the stretcher and tie you in. Don't try to help. Let us do the lifting. You just relax, okay?"

Pete nodded. Vance lived his shoulders and back onto the stretcher, while Henri moved his hips and legs.

"Yow..."

"Sorry." Henri felt for his friend, but moving him onto the stretcher couldn't be helped. He strapped Pete down and tied the canvas cover over him.

Letting him rest for a minute, Henri watched Pete's face. His eyes were half closed. Henri realized Pete was trying to hold back the rising pain. "Pain getting to be too much?" Pete nodded. Henri opened his bag and pulled out the morphine and a needle. After he gave Pete a shot, he waited until he saw the pain die out of his eyes. "Now, listen. We're going to lower you over the side. The doctor is waiting for you and so is your father. Remember do not move! We'll try to keep you level. This bag will hold and we won't let you fall. Got it?"

"Got it." Pete attempted a grin. "You have a bloody good bedside manner, doc," he said, imitating Henri's English accent.

"Good man. We'll see you a little later."

Henri and Vance lowered Pete over the side, bracing themselves against the dead weight, letting him down slowly until Henri felt the rope slacken. Both sat down on the ledge for a few minutes rest and until they felt two signal tugs on the rope. With an effort, Henri pulled himself to his feet, helping Vance haul the stretcher back up the cliff.

The two men slowly and carefully worked their way to the next ledge where Pete had told them Burt was lying.

"There he is!" Vance shouted, "and look...just over there…on that ledge to the right…it's Mario!"

"Thank God," Henri whispered.

The ledge on which Burt lay unconscious was mercifully a little wider than the one below giving them more room in which to work. Henri could get no response from Burt. He checked his pulse and, as he had with Pete, ran his hands over Burt's body checking for broken bones.

"Three ribs are broken," he said, sitting back on his heels, a puzzled frown creasing his forehead. Glancing up at Vance Henri added, "Nothing else appears wrong." He gently probed Burt's skull. His face froze. "That's why!"

"What?"

"He's got a concussion."

"Oh, hell!"

Vance held Burt's head steady while Henri put a neck brace around the injured man's neck. Working fast, they strapped him onto the stretcher. Henri quickly wrote a note and tied it to the stretcher to alert the doctor. Burt's fifteen plus stone weight threatened to drag Henri and Vance over the side, but they steeled themselves calling upon unknown reserves of strength, lowered him safely. Henri knew the exertion had taken more out of him than he had hoped and, even with Vance's help, his remaining strength continued to slip away and he wasn't sure how much he could rely on his shrinking reserves. Henri had to make a choice now of getting Mario or of getting himself and Vance down. Two tugs brought his thoughts up with a jerk. He pulled himself to his feet, hauled the stretcher back up and knowing in his heart there really was no choice, moved cautiously toward the ledge on which Mario lay.

The sun had begun to dip toward the horizon shedding its hazy cold late afternoon light on the Eagle's Nest when Henri and Vance lowered themselves onto the ledge and turned to meet Mario's eyes. "Good afternoon," Henri said cheerfully with a smile. "You chaps had quite a time for yourselves up here. How are you feeling?"

Mario smiled back weakly, "I never thought I would say it's good to see you, but it is. I gather we failed our exercise miserably and will have to climb this damned cliff again to make up. To use one of your English phrases, blast the bloody luck!" He gave Henri a quizzical look, "What made you come up here?"

"Well, it seems Vance and I are the only experienced rock climbers, other than yourselves, north of Wales, so it was up to us to get you down." Henri grinned as he moved his hands over Mario. "Don't worry about failing. It happens to the best of us. Have you any broken bones?"

"I'm not sure. I think my left arm is and I twisted my back rather badly."

"Right." Henri began to check, splint and bandage Mario.

A few small rocks bounced off the ledge. Both Vance and Henri swiftly scanned the cliff above them, their faces tense. *Dear God, don't let a slide start now!* Henri silently prayed.

When nothing more happened, Henri and Vance strapped Mario in quickly. "Listen to me carefully. We are going to lower you down and I do not want you to move. The doctor is waiting for you and your father also. Don't worry, the ropes are fairly new and we'll not let you fall. I know this bag will hold for you. It held Burt," Henri said with a grin. "Right then. Any questions?"

"No, lower away Captain," and as Henri and Vance lifted him over the side, he said quietly, his dark eyes serious, "By the way, thanks."

Henri grinned again and nodded his head. Gently they let him down, again praying a rockslide would not start. When they felt the ropes go slack, the signal Mario was safe, the two men sank down on the ledge with their back against the cliff, exhausted.

After about fifteen minutes, Vance and Henri looked at each other and nodded. "Shall we haul the stretcher up?" Vance asked.

Henri thought for a moment, "I guess we'd better. We may need the ropes attached to it."

"Better safe than sorry?" This time it was Vance who grinned.

"Right."

When the stretcher was up, Vance said, "Okay, I'll lead off this time." Carefully, they moved off the ledge, Vance heading for the small ledge on which they had found Pete, but just as he reached it, the rock under his foot gave way and Vance felt his body falling through space.

Henri looked down in horror, automatically bracing himself to take the sharp jerk when Vance reached the end of the rope tied between them.

Vince's agonized scream echoed over the mountain. His left shoulder sent a stab of pain racing through his body as the force of the jerking stop to his fall tore it out of its socket. Now a little below the ledge, swinging helplessly over the void, terror overcame pain.

Nearly jerked from his position, Henri had managed to hang on. "I'm going to try to reach the ledge. Then I can haul you up," he shouted. "Try to get a secure hold, and then don't move until I say to."

"Concentrate," Vance whispered to himself. "Focus." He reached out gingerly. His fingertips touched rock. He swallowed hard and grasped firmly with his right hand, pain surged through his right foot, but he found purchase with the toes of his left foot against the solid rock wall. "Okay...Okay...I think I'm secure now."

After feeling Vance's weight ease up on the rope, Henri began to inch down until he reached the ledge. "I'm going to start pulling you up."

"I can't use my left arm and, somehow, I twisted my right ankle. I'll try to give you as much help as I can."

"Here goes." Using all the strength he had, Henri pulled Vance inch-by-inch up the cliff.

Vance felt with his right hand for every crevice or protruding rock to help but he was weakening fast from the pain in his shoulder. It seemed like hours of struggling, before he felt Henri grab his wrist and with a final heave, pull him up onto the ledge. Vance closed his eyes and his mind went blank.

At the point of complete exhaustion, Henri knew he couldn't give in. Marshaling every ounce of strength, he pulled Vance's boot off and had almost completed with bandaging the ankle when Vance opened his eyes. "How long have I been out?"

"Not long."

"Okay. Now what?"

"First, I'm going to help you sit up, and then I'm going to get your shoulder back into its socket."

"And how the hell are you going to do that?"

"I'll show you. Now sit up."

With Henri's help, Vance sat up, leaning back against the cliff.

"Okay. This is going to hurt like hell, but only for a couple of seconds."

"It already hurts like hell. Why not leave it the way it is until I get down to the doctor?"

"If you leave it dislocated for too long, the doctor would have to operate and you'll have more trouble in the future. In addition, you'll have to endure the pain much longer. Once I get your shoulder back into place, you won't have any more pain. Trust me."

"Okay."

"Now listen carefully. I'm going to put my left hand under your elbow and hold your wrist with my right hand. Okay?"

"Yeah."

"There are three steps to this process. First, I'm going to straighten your arm out slightly to the side; then, keeping your wrist out, I'm going to pull your elbow across your chest. I'm going to have to pull hard enough so the top of the bone will come in line with the socket and start to slide into it. When it does, I will fold your wrist up and over toward your right shoulder. Your arm will go back where it ought to be. Got it?"

"Yeah. Go ahead. Haul away."

Henri grinned. "Try not to move. Brace yourself against the cliff. I'll do it as fast as I can."

As soon as Henri began to move his arm, Vince bit back a scream. Mercifully, the procedure was over quickly. Once the shoulder was back in place, Henri sat back on his heels. "You all right?"

"Yeah. I'm fine." Vance laughed. "Hey, what do you know, there's no pain!"

"Good. Now I'm going to strap your arm to your chest so you won't be able to dislocate the shoulder again."

"How the hell are we going to get down if I can't use my arm?"

"I'm going to lower you in the stretcher."

"Henri, you can't!"

"What else do you propose?"

"Wait for another rescue team."

"Vance, do you see those clouds over there?"

"Yeah."

"Those are storm clouds. It took us a good three hours to get up here and you and I are far more experienced than anyone else. That storm is going to hit us within two hours at the least. We can't survive up here without shelter. You can't even rappel down, let alone climb. I'm going to have to get you down on my own and the only way is to lower you on the stretcher."

"You aren't strong enough to hold my full weight plus the weight of the stretcher!"

"I can fix the ropes so I can break them. I'll lower you feet first by fits and starts. At least I can get you down before the storm hits."

"What about you?" You'll be up here exposed to the full force of the storm."

"Look, Vance. I'm not hurt. I can get down fast by rappelling, you can't! You would pull your shoulder out again and we would be back were we started." He glanced at the clouds. "Make up your mind fast. We don't have much time."

Vance knew Henri was right. He also knew that Henri wouldn't leave him if he decided to take his chances and stay. He really had no choice and was going to have to trust Henri. "Okay. What do you want me to do?"

Swiftly Henri tied Vance in the bag and onto the stretcher, making sure all the ropes were in place. "This bag will hold and I won't let you fall, Vance, I promise. Don't worry. You will slip down a little and I want you to even your weight so the stretcher doesn't lean to one side or the other. Look ahead or up, but don't look down. You will only get dizzy if you do. Got it?"

"Got it!"

"I'll see you below." Henri carefully tipped the stretcher over the side and prayed. He felt the ropes pull taught as Vance's full weight almost dragged Henri over the side. Little by little he allowed the stretcher to descend, his arms burning with the effort. The pain was so intense he feared his own shoulders would slip out of their sockets. After what seemed an eternity, he felt the ropes go slack and knew Vance was safely down.

Henri sank down on the ledge, his back against the cliff, completely exhausted. A cold wind started up while he rested, regaining his strength. Heavy, dark clouds scudded across the sky and the little warmth from the sun was fading fast. He had no idea how long he sat there, but realized he must have dozed off. His legs were cramped, but he still had no strength to move. All he wanted was to lie down and sleep, but this, he knew, would be fatal. Still he did not move.

Lazily, he watched two majestic birds flying in slow circles, soaring on the air currents above him. *This place is aptly named the "Eagle's Nest,"* he thought, idly gazing out over the rolling countryside covered in its white blanket, with the river glinting cold grey, snaking through it.

Looking down over the camp below, he wished he could fly like the two birds above him. *It would be so easy. All I would have to do is just step off this ledge. Then I could float down and down until I landed on that soft cushion of powdered snow below.*

He shook his head and brought these dangerous thoughts up abruptly, as his narrowed veiled eyes suddenly focused on a large round black patch near the medical tent. It had a familiar look, but his tired mind did not register what it was for a few minutes; then he realized it was the yurt. He laughed out loud as he pictured General Dayton watching this exotic relic of a long dead past materialize next to his neat modern army tent.

Slowly, with every muscle screaming, Henri dragged his aching body to its feet to begin the long climb down. Slowly,

slowly, inches at a time, getting a toe hold on a ledge, a grip with his hand on an outcropping, he stopped frequently to rest before going on.

"Crack!" His head jerked up as above him he heard a noise as sharp as that of a rifle. "Dear God, help me," he whispered, swiftly wrapping the ropes around his gloved hands, pressing his body against the cliff. He tried to cover his head with his arms as rocks fell all around him. Some hit the ropes, making them vibrate like violin strings. One bounced off his shoulder, another his temple. He lost his foothold and dangled full length, bumping against the cliff side. Desperately, he hung onto a jutting rock, his arms stretched out completely, his body swinging side to side..

Henri hung there for what seemed hours. Only when the stillness folded back around him and he heard the cry of a hawk did he realize the slide was over. "Thank you, Father," he whispered, closing his eyes in silent prayer. Carefully, he searched for a toe-hold to ease his aching arms. It was obvious he was going to have to rappel since he had no strength to work his way step by step anymore, and if he was going to get down alive, he had to do it fast.

Stiffly, he shifted the ropes and leaned away from the cliff to start down again. His mind, blank from exhaustion, he forced himself to think about, and will, every step he took. Once, feeling below him with his left foot, he put his weight on a piece of rock when suddenly the rock fell away from the cliff. His left leg skidded out from under him and his shoulders wrenched causing his arms to take the full weight of his body, breaking his fall. Pain shot through him. He felt the ligaments tear in his bad arm, making it useless for further rappelling.

Desperately, he searched for a toehold again, found it and, using only one leg and arm, improvising as best he could, he slowly, painfully started down again. Blackness swept over him in waves. He had no strength left. His one good arm held the full weight of his body and his grasp on the rope was weakening. Desperately, he hung on, his tired mind searching for a way out. Glancing down he saw a narrow ledge just below him. *If I can reach that ledge, I can tie myself onto it and maybe, just maybe survive the storm.*

With the last of his strength, Henri maneuvered his pain ridden body to the ledge. Sprawled full length on its rough surface, the final waves of black exhaustion swept over him.

Paul and Alexei prepared to climb the cliff as soon as they arrived at the campsite. Although, Henri didn't know it, they were already three quarters of the way up the cliff at the time he collapsed.

Seeing him, they swiftly worked their way up to the ledge where he lay unconscious. "Thank God he was this side of the slide. A few more feet over and he would have been dead," Paul said, securely tying himself to his rope so that he had both hands free.

Alexei, close beside him, worked himself to the other side of the ledge. "Umm. We're still too close for comfort."

Gently, Paul lifted Henri's inert body, turning him over. "We're going to have to carry him down. Damn! We should have brought the stretcher with us. No matter. Alexei, give me that extra rope you brought."

As the rope began to slide under Henri's inert body, he stirred and opened his eyes. At first, he was only vaguely aware of his uncle's presence, and then his mind began to clear. Tiredly, he smiled up at Paul. "Thank you for coming up after me."

"How badly off are you, Henri?"

"I've pulled the ligaments in my arm and my left leg is useless and, of course, I'm totally exhausted."

"All right, I'll tie you between Alexei and me with a safety rope. Between us with your help, I think we can get you down."

With Paul's help, Henri stood up on the ledge and Paul and Alexei securely roped him to themselves. The cold wind had increased in strength. Now, it pinned the three men against the cliff. The sky had turned a thunderous black obscuring the setting sun. The first stinging needles of snow hit them and they all knew they had to get down quickly before the main part of the storm hit.

The effort of standing, together with the increased cold were too much. Henri's mind went blank again. Later, he had no memory of the terrifying trip down. He collapsed between the two men several times, but the ropes held and his uncle and cousin were able to carry his weight. At the bottom of the mountain, he began to regain his senses and felt two strong hands clasp his waist. Igor's familiar voice came to his ears. "I've got you, your Highness, just one more step and you will be on solid ground."

Henri leaned against the cliff, his forehead pressed against its cold, rough surface, while a strong arm held him on his left. Turning, he met Igor's eyes. Henri's head dropped against Igor's shoulder as his longtime servant and friend held him in his arms.

Alexei threw a familiar long fur-lined cloak around Henri's shoulders and Igor picked him up and carried him toward the medical tent.

After Dr. White examined him and put his arm in a sling, Igor carried him across the clearing to the yurt against Henri's mumbled protest, "I can walk, Igor. I can walk."

"Tomorrow. You can walk tomorrow."

Henri slept the rest of that night and all the next day, not even waking when the storm broke, raging around the tent.

"You did a fine job on yourself up there." Dr. White helped Henri back into his Russian blouse, adjusting his arm in the sling. "Every time you hurt your bad leg or arm—and it's always the bad ones—you weaken them more and it takes longer for them to heal."

"Sorry about that, but I couldn't avoid it." Henri grinned, as he awkwardly tucked the blouse inside his black riding trousers. This was his first day up since the rescue and he had been permitted to wear civilian clothes while he was with his family.

"At ease, Bolkonsky, carry on," General Dayton said, as he entered the room. "The men were asking for you this morning. I think they would like to see you."

"Do you know about what, sir?" Henri warily raised one eyebrow, already guessing the answer.

"I believe they would like to thank you for getting them off the cliff. Their fathers would too, for that matter," Dayton replied.

Henri shifted uncomfortably under the general's gaze, "I don't need any thanks, sir, besides I wasn't the only one. Vance was there too."

"They have already thanked him, You'll have to face them sometime and you might as well do it now. They know you are here, so when you finish, I suggest you go in to see them." The general watched Henri in amusement.

"How is Vance, doctor?" Henri asked. "Is he in the room with the others?"

"No, I released him to go back with his group. He told me you fixed his shoulder." Dr. White smiled. "You did a good job. How did you know how to snap it back into place?"

Henri shrugged. "A friend of mine showed me how. He was a medical student and showed me a lot of things that have come in handy."

"I see."

It took longer for Henri to dress than usual. Finally ready, he glanced around but saw no escape. Both the general and the doctor were watching him. Straightening his shoulders, he gave them a somewhat shy smile, picked up the heavy fur-lined cloak, hesitated, and walked through the flap into the area where the three men waited with their fathers and several Academy friends. With a slight smile, he said, "Well, you're all looking cheerful. Welcome to the land of the living, Burt. How is that bump on your head?"

Burt gave him a wry grin, "Other than a headache, I'm fine."

"Good, I'm glad to hear it. When will you be able to box again, Mario?"

"Not until next fall but it doesn't matter, I need to concentrate on my studies anyway. How are you feeling?"

"Much better after that long sleep." He stood just inside the room, one hand in his pocket, now he sauntered over to stand by Pete's bed. "How's the leg?"

"It'll have to stay in a cast for a while, but that shouldn't slow me down much."

Burt's father broke in, "Mr. Bolkonsky, all of us want to thank you for saving our sons' lives. There are really no words with which to do it, nor any way we can repay you." His sincere gruff voice stopped. He didn't know what else to say, and the level gaze of the blue eyes now turned on him was disconcerting. With a gentle smile, Henri replied, "No thanks necessary. Someday they

64

may be in a position to save someone else and that will be repayment enough." "I must join my family now. I'll see all of you later." He turned to the door, but as he raised the flap to leave, a deep voice stopped him. "It appears that the McGovern family owes you two lives." Henri turned slowly to face Bruce McGovern. "You not only saved my oldest son's life, but now my youngest. I owe you a great deal." The elder McGovern said in his quiet drawl.

"You don't owe me anything, Mr. McGovern."

"I can't agree with you, Henri. Whether you like it or not you are owed thanks and don't give me your standard answer."

Dave McGovern entered through the flap and put his hand on Henri's good shoulder.

"Dave! It's good to see you," Henri said with genuine pleasure. "I didn't know you were up here."

"It's good to see you again, too, and to know you're alive. Pete wrote to me about you, but I didn't believe it was the same person."

Henri shrugged his shoulders with an amused twinkle in his eyes, "You know I have a reputation of being indestructible."

"I know your reputation, but that doesn't mean that you *are* indestructible. I won't be side-tracked this time. We owe you a great deal. "Dave's face was serious, but his mouth quirked up at the corners in amusement.

The shy smile returned as Henri shook his head. He said nothing but moved uncomfortably under Dave's gaze, now a wide smile in amusement. "Don't look so damned embarrassed. Okay. Okay. I'll let you escape gracefully."

Henri's smile this time was grateful as he backed toward the flap. "Come over to the yurt for a drink this evening and we can talk," he said, then with a slight bow taking in everyone in the room, made his retreat.

"He seemed genuinely embarrassed," Leonardo said in amazement. "God! If it had been me, I would have sat there basking in all the praise and thanks."

"He was embarrassed and he has never expected thanks. He thinks of it as part of his responsibility," Dave shrugged with a laugh. "Well you heard his standard answer, but believe, me, he means every word of it."

"What do you mean by 'his responsibility'?" Dave's father asked.

Dave thought for a minute before replying, "Henri considers himself one of the lucky ones of this world. He wants for nothing. He was born with the proverbial silver spoon in his mouth and he need never lift a finger to work, if he doesn't want to. But he believes he was born into this life for a reason, blessed with the abilities he has and his unbelievable luck. He believes he must use those abilities to help others."

"Greater love hath no man than this, that a man lay down his life for his friends," Guido murmured the quotation.

Dave shot him a quick smile. "No, more like: I am my brother's keeper. It's hard to put into words, even Henri has never really attempted to do so, as far as I know."

"How do you know he believes this, if he has never said so?" Leonardo asked.

"He doesn't really have to say it…his actions and his whole life say it for him," Dave answered quickly. "All I know is that he's quite a guy…one of the greatest in my book."

Henri emerged from the yurt that afternoon after lunch and stood scanning the sky. A slight wind caught at the hem of his cloak, otherwise, the sky was clear, not a cloud in sight. The sun was warm and the heavy snow from the night before lay thick on the ground. He smiled as Alexei brought a group of horses around the corner of the tent.

"Hola!" Henri called. "Wait a minute and I'll join you. I have to check with the doctor first, but I'll be right back."

"Right. I'll wait, but don't be too long."

Henri strode, limping slightly, across the clearing to the medical tent. Dr. White and General Dayton stood talking with two other men whom Henri didn't recognize. The doctor looked up as he approached. "How are the arm and leg this afternoon?"

"Fine except for the fact I can hardly move with these bloody bandages restricting me. I feel as if I'm encased in a suit of armor; otherwise, everything is all right."

66

"Good, let me check the arm again." The doctor took Henri's arm out of the sling and, holding it out straight, started to raise it slowly.

"Careful, it still hurts," Henri winced, a slight frown appearing on his face. "How long are we staying here?"

"I don't want to move the other three men for another day. I think you had better stay with your family rather than return to your group today as you had planned."

"Why?" Henri looked sharply at the doctor.

"You will be more comfortable here for one thing and closer to me for another." White made his voice sound casual, adding, "The rest I think had better come from General Dayton."

Henri tensed, turning to face the general. Alert and now suspicious and on his guard, he raised one eyebrow?

"These gentlemen are from M15, Mr. Bolkonsky. They have just brought word that a certain Colonel von Kant has slipped into Scotland from Denmark. He has been seen in this vicinity and they believe he may be up here looking for you."

A far-away look came into Henri's eyes as a slow, cold smile spread across his now masked face. Very softly, musingly, he breathed, "So they sent the old Grey Wolf."

"Do you know him, Mr.Bolkonsky?" General Dayton asked sharply.

"Yes, very well. He's an old opponent, though I have never actually had the pleasure of meeting him." The strange flickering light came into his eyes. "It's going to be very interesting to see who finishes this part of the hunt."

Chapter 7

"I think, Mr. Bolkonsky, it would be safer for you to stay with your family while we are encamped here."

"It may be safer for me, but more dangerous for them. Actually, it would be still harder for them to spot me amongst the troops."

"That is not exactly true," one of the agents commented. "You and your cousins look alike, are the same height and wear the same type of clothes. They will not be able to tell one from the other."

Henri whirled on him, anger tingeing his voice," I do not want my family hurt; that is why I agreed to come here in the first place. They will just pick us off one by one to make sure they have gotten me. No, I would rather take my chances out in the open and keep my family safe."

As the general was framing a reply to this argument, a shot rang out. Before its echoes died away, Henri had dropped to the ground disappearing around the corner of the tent. With the tent shielding his movements, he sprinted as fast as he could for the woods surrounding the clearing. He unclasped his heavy cloak and left it lying in the snow like a blot of ink on clean white paper.

He stopped just inside the first edge of trees. Their branches hung low, weighted down by heavy snow. Snow half covered the underbrush at the edge of the woods but further in, the brush thinned and the ground was clearer. Branches met overhead in an almost impenetrable tangle letting in no sunlight. Henri shivered in the gloomy cold.

He moved forward cautiously circling toward the spot where the shot had been fired. His eyes became accustomed to the dusk in the woods as he moved from tree to tree like a shadow. He could hear muddled orders being given from the camp and knew the general was setting up a dragnet.

A twig snapped behind him. He whirled, a knife appearing in his hand as if produced out of the air. Standing behind the bole of an ancient tree, he listened to the stealthy progress of two men. He sprang forward, his knife raised ready to strike as the first man passed him. He checked the descent just in time as Alexei whirled to face him, his gun raised.

"You bloody damned idiots. What the hell are you doing here?" Facing Alexei and his Uncle Paul, Henri's voice was rough with anger and fear at his almost fatal mistake.

"Doing a spot of hunting." Alexei's smile was half mocking, half serious.

"We have no idea how many men are in these woods, so we thought we would come to your assistance, if you needed it."

Again Henri whirled. In his surprise he had forgotten the second set of footsteps he had heard. Now he looked into his uncle's eyes. He knew from past experience, it would be useless to try to persuade them to go back to the camp where it was safe. He simply nodded his head. "Right, but I heard you coming. For God's sake, try to move more silently."

Paul smiled. "I brought along an extra gun for you, thought you might not have one and would need it."

Henri grinned. "Thanks." He slipped the knife back into its soft sheath strapped to his wrist.

"Where do you think your friends are now? This is a hell of a big woods." Alexei broke in impatiently.

"The shot came from somewhere between the medical tent and ours, behind where I was standing. I should imagine Colonel von Kant and whoever is with him are circling in this direction.

"Great. So we have no idea where they are. We can't cover this entire woods and we don't even have a trail to follow."

"Where is the general starting his dragnet, Uncle Paul?" Henri turned to his uncle, disregarding Alexei's remark.

"I believe on a line roughly from just below our tent to the cliff and sweeping in this direction."

"Right. I'll have to presume that Colonel von Kant and his man will stay somewhat close to the edge of the woods to look for me. I don't think he'll believe I've gone very deep inside."

"Why?" Alexei asked.

"Because the cover is not good further in. There are too many gaps where he could get a good clear shot, whereas here at the edge, I have a lot more cover. Also he may think that, if by chance I made a break for the tents, he would have a good shot."

"Since he didn't see you run toward or into the woods, he may think you are still around the tents."

"That's another point I hadn't thought of. I doubt it, Uncle Paul, but you may be right."

"Well, most people run from danger or stay where it's safe, they rarely run toward it."

Henri looked at Paul. "Where is Jean?"

"I ordered him and Igor to stay in the yurt and guard the women." As he talked, Paul kept scanning the woods. "von Kant will eventually see your tracks in the snow as well as ours."

"You're right and that's why we're going to circle further inside the woods where we'll be able to see them more quickly than they'll see us. We'll be in the gloom, but they'll be outlined against the backdrop of the snow."

"Right. Let's find cover before they get here.

Three men backtracked in the direction from which they had come. When they reached the point where they had entered the woods, they turned deeper into the gloom of the trees. Henri began to move more cautiously, for he knew Colonel von Kant should be fairly close behind now. When he judged they had penetrated deeply enough, he again turned in the direction from which he expected Colonel von Kant to approach them..

Nothing disturbed the tranquility of the woods. Occasionally, the soft plop of heavy snow falling from high branches reached their ears. Once, Henri saw a startled bird flit through the trees. Tracks of a few wild animals crisscrossed their path but nothing stirred in the silence. Overhead, the trees looked black. Henri and Alexei would have enjoyed the mysterious tranquil beauty of these woods if their errand had not been so desperate.

70

Henri estimated they had reached the spot near where he had met Alexei and Paul. The men had seen no sign of Colonel von Kant or of anyone with him. "They couldn't have passed us without our knowing," Henri said, as they paused for a minute. I propose we keep going until we reach the spot where the shot was fired. If we don't see them before then, we might be able to pick up their tracks there and follow them."

"Good idea." Paul nodded.

"What if they've given up for now and disappeared? By this time, they must know we're hunting them and General Dayton's dragnet must have started through the woods. They could have been frightened off."

"I doubt that, Alexei, knowing Colonel von Kant. I think he's still here lying low. He's a good hunter and knows all the tricks of the woods," Henri smiled, "but so do we. At least we stand an even chance.

They started off again moving silently over the damp earth. Each slipped from tree to tree straining their ears for the slightest sound, their eyes ever searching ahead and to each side. Henri, the more experienced of the three in stalking men, relied as much on his ever-alert instincts as upon his sight and hearing. Every muscle and nerve in his body was ready to react to the slightest scent of danger.

Ahead, they heard the sounds of the dragnet coming toward them. Henri stopped, motioning Alexei and Paul to join him. "The dragnet has passed the point where the shot was fired, so my calculations must be wrong. Colonel von Kant has done one of two things. He's moved deeper into the woods and by-passed us as we were coming this way or he's taken the risk and is now amongst the tents in the clearing where I was."

"I doubt he took that risk, Henri. It's far too dangerous and would jeopardize his whole mission. There are too many people around those tents and, unless he is prepared to kill everyone he meets, which in itself is risky, he would not have gone in that direction."

"I'm inclined to agree with you, von Kant is no fool."

"I think we should head deeper into the woods," Paul said. "We may come across his tracks there. Do you know of any footpath or dirt road through here?"

"No, but there is very likely to be one."

"Well, lead on MacDuff," Alexei quipped waiting to start off in the new direction.

Henri and Paul looked at each other with half amused smiles. Alexei took danger much more lightly than Henri, as he also took life. Paul watched his son and his nephew, both the same age and both much the same in looks, but so different in many ways in temperament. He could never make up his mind which of them had chosen the better road.

The men moved parallel to each other about ten feet apart. They kept each other in sight at all times as they went forward. A clearing appeared straight ahead of Henri, covered with several feet of snow. The sky above had turned a leaden grey. A soft soughing wind blew through the tops of the trees sending small flurries of snow down through the heavily laden branches. Paul, in the center of the three, would just miss the far edge of the clearing and Alexei, on the other side would not see it at all. Henri slowed his pace even more as he cautiously moved up to its edge.

While he stood, partially hidden by the brush and trees, studying the ground, he caught a stealthy movement slightly to his right on the opposite side of the clearing. He froze watching the spot intently. Then a tall powerfully built man stepped from the shelter of the trees. He was almost as tall as Henri with blond hair and light blue eyes. A dueling scar ran the full length of one cheek. He was broad shouldered and slim hipped and, like Henri, Paul and Alexei, wore riding clothes, his brown boots shining even with the overcast sky. He typified the aristocratic Prussian officer of the old school. He carried a rifle in the crook of his arm, pointed toward the ground, but ready to be brought into action instantly.

Henri glanced to his left. Paul had turned back and was coming toward him. He motioned slightly with his hand for him to be quiet. Paul nodded and, followed by Alexei, turned a little deeper into the woods in order to approach Henri and the clearing without being seen.

Henri turned back toward the clearing and saw that another man had joined the Colonel. Henri assumed he was the Colonel's aide, Captain Hardt. A little shorter than von Kant and with light brown hair, he also was dressed in riding clothes and carried a Luger in his belt. Much younger than his superior officer, he had the same air about him. The two stood in the clearing under the lowering grey sky quietly conferring.

"Humm. Not quite as formidable as I thought." Paul's quiet voice reached Henri from behind his shoulder.

"No, but formidable enough." Henri's eyes narrowed slightly. "There do not seem to be any others with him. I could be wrong, but I don't think so. Colonel von Kant usually works alone with only his aide captain Hardt."

"All right. Alexei and I can circle around, so that we can approach the clearing from three sides."

"No. It would take you too long. By that time von Kant and Hardt could be gone."

"True, but it's still better to be scattered than in a group. They are less likely to hit one of us."

The two men in the clearing turned sharply, listening. At the same moment, Henri heard the same sounds they did. The troops were approaching. Taking advantage of von Kant and Hardt's backs turned to them, Henri stepped swiftly into the open with Paul and Alexei on either side, their guns raised.

"Your quest is finished Colonel von Kant," Henri said in German in a flat cold voice. "I would suggest you drop your guns and turn around slowly. It would be very hard to miss you from this distance."

Colonel von Kant's half-turned back stiffened at the first sound of Henri's voice. Henri stood tense, waiting, until to his relief, he saw the Colonel lower his rifle, gently placing it on the ground. Captain Hardt, who had stood like a statue and whose back remained turned, moved his hand slowly to his belt. With a sudden snake-like movement, he drew the Lugar out, turned and fired. Henri felt the wind of the bullet as it passed close to his ear. Three other guns fired simultaneously with Hardt's. The gun flew from his hand and a red splotch appeared on the right shoulder of his immaculate jacket.

At the first sound of fired guns, Colonel von Kant dropped to the ground rolling toward the nearby edge of the clearing. Before any of them could fire another shot, he disappeared into the brush and trees and was gone. "Come on, Alexei," Henri called, as he raced into the woods to try to cut off von Kant's retreat. Although Paul remained in the clearing to look after their wounded prisoner, his first reaction was to follow his son and nephew.

Henri ducked under the branches of the first line of trees, but instinctively slowed his pace. He didn't know if Colonel von Kant had another gun, but it seemed most likely that he did. He stopped to listen and Alexei almost bumped into him. The woods were as still as ever, the only noise the approach of the troops as they hurried toward the sound of the shots. They were near now. Much too near, Henri thought, for him to hear any sound that might betray his quarry.

He and Alexei moved at a slight angle away from the clearing and away from the dragnet, going deeper into the woods. The gloom had deepened as the afternoon wore on. Darkness was descending quickly. They had to find von Kant within the next hour; otherwise, he would slip away altogether. Silently, the two men worked their way from tree to tree, ears straining for any sound, eyes straining for any movement. Alexei again moved off to Henri's side about ten feet away. Small showers of snow quietly drifted down on them as the cold penetrating wind stirred the branches.

Suddenly, Henri felt the gun knocked from his hand and von Kant was on him, his knife gleaming as he thrust it toward Henri's chest. In an instant, he held his own knife in his hand as he simultaneously threw himself sideways. The colonel's gleaming steel missed Henri by a fraction of an inch. Colonel von Kant checked himself, turned in a flash and swung the knife again, close …too close…to Henri's body. Henri leaped backward parrying the blow with his own knife blade. Tearing the sling from around his neck for greater freedom, he felt the ligaments in his arm scream in protest. He had no time to think about it for von Kant was on top of him again. Again the blade just missed him as he whirled out of the way slashing at the Colonel.

Alexei tried to get a clear shot, but it was useless in the brush and trees. He was afraid he would hit Henri instead. Thrusting his gun into his belt, he leaped at the two struggling men and grabbed the Colonel's arm as he brought the knife in an upward thrust. The Colonel broke away whirling on him as Alexei swiftly backed off pulling his gun from his belt. For a tense moment while Alexei held the gun on von Kant, he wasn't sure if the Colonel would try to throw his knife in one last attempt to get Henri. If his hatred of Henri was sufficient to make him suicidal, the split second before Alexei could fire at him was all the Colonel would need to kill Henri.

Slowly, imperceptibly, von Kant's arm relaxed, the point of his knife tipping toward the ground. Henri spoke for the first time. "Lower your gun, Alexei," he commanded, then turned bleak eyes toward the Colonel. "Go now. The General and his troops will be here in a few minutes. Go back to your home and your family. The war is over and they need you." His voice held an unutterable weariness.

Looking between the two cousins, von Kant nodded, saying softly, "The old Grey Wolf will return to his lair and will not hunt again."

"I'll see that your weapons are returned to you with Captain Hardt. Go now."

With a strange smile upon his lips, Colonel von Kant said musingly, "What dam of Lances brought thee forth to jest at the dawn with death?" For a moment longer he looked at Henri, then clicking his heels, bowed and disappeared into the gathering dusk of the woods.

Henri stood by Alexei's side staring at the place where the Colonel had gone, softly he replied, "I hold by the blood of my clan."

Paul appeared at his side, relief plainly written on his face, he touched Henri's arm. He had come upon the little group silently and had seen and heard the end of the battle. He understood why Henri had let the Colonel go. Wearily, Henri turned and slowly the three men walked back to join the troop and the family.

That night, General Dayton and Dr. White were invited for dinner with the family in the yurt. A cold wind came up in the early evening and as the night wore on, seemed to gather in fury. It beat at the sides of the tent, swept over its rounded black sides; snatched at the smoke which rose through the center hole at the top, seemingly wanting to blow the tent and all its occupants across the hills.

Inside, it was warm. Braziers cast red shadows on heavy woolen curtains which shut each section of the tent off. Dinner— an Indonesian Ristaffel with its many different meats, pork and chicken dishes in various delicious spiced sauces—was cooked and served by Pyotr and Igor.

As the men sat back in chairs replete and satisfied, the last dishes were removed. One curtain was raised revealing another area of the tent which served as a living room for the family. Igor brought in coffee and Alicia poured.

Alexei, lacking his father's understanding, turned to Henri, "Why did you let Colonel von Kant go today? He would have killed you and yet you turned him loose."

"I don't know, Alexei," Henri said wearily. "I'm tired of killing. The war is over and his death would have been meaningless. There was no real need. You stayed your hand when you had a clear shot. Why?"

"I suppose because he had given up," Alexei replied slowly.

"Just so. As I said, there was no real need to kill him. Life is too precious to waste it. There has been enough…too much…blood shed already."

"But, why let him go? You could have turned him over to General Dayton," Alexei persisted.

"To what purpose? To be put in prison?" Henri shook his head. "No, Alexei. He hunted me all during the war and we have matched wits for too long. He had great courage and is an intelligent leader. I respect him too much to let him languish in prison, besides his family needs his strength to rebuild what has been destroyed."

"I think I get it." Alexei turned to Paul, "I remember you telling a story with a similar ending, Papa, something that happened in Russia…"

Paul nodded and filled his pipe thoughtfully before responding, "Yes, The Civil War had started and I had been bitterly fighting my arch-enemy at the time, a quick intelligent young man, Chevsky. After a lengthy exhausting fight, with one quick slash I disarmed him. I raised my saber, but instead of the expected swing that would mean his death, I threw my saber down point first into the ground where it quivered between us." He paused. "Do not ask me why, for I cannot tell you. Perhaps, it was the way he stood there, his head held erect, unafraid. I do not know. I never saw him again, but I have often thought of him. He was a very brave man."

Later that night, as General Dayton and Dr. White walked back across the clearing, the general remarked, "You know all those people were poured out of the same mold, even Colonel von Kant and his Aide. They come from a school that is fast dying out and yet fortunately, they have passed on some of their values to their young. God help this world if their kind become completely extinct."

"I'll say amen to that," Dr. White replied.

Chapter 8

"Hey, Bolkonsky, you'd better get down to the stables quick!" Larry called as he dashed along the path to meet Henri.

"Why?" Henri grinned. He already had guessed the reason since he could hear the commotion in the stable yard.

"Your horse has arrived and is raising holy hell down there."

"So Uncle Paul managed to find someone to transport him. Good." Henri quickened his pace.

"Some idiot to transport him is more like it. He's trying to kick down the sides of the trailer, and the stable hand is frightened out of his wits," Larry said somewhat out of breath.

"Damn! That will only make him worse." Henri rounded the end of the stables and saw that the man had been able to back Vlaska down the ramp and into the open.

The big stallion reared, lashing out with sharp hooves, his ears back. His jet-black coat gleamed in the sun and the white mane, tail and forelock tossed wildly about. Henri stepped quickly through the crowd that had gathered at a respectful distance from the horse. Grabbing the halter rope in his hand, he swiftly vaulted to Vlaska's back. The horse, surprised at the liberty taken, whirled around in a tight circle. He reared again while his rider gently stroked his neck, speaking in a low soothing voice. Vlaska could not dislodge Henri no matter how hard he tried. Finally, the great stallion tired and stood still tossing his head in frustration, his ears twitching listening to his rider's soft voice. Henri slid off his back still stroking Vlaska's arched neck and continuing to speak to him in the same soothing voice.

Captain Harding, the head riding master who had been watching the whole performance, came up with what could only be construed as a resounding understatement, "He seems a bit wild."

A quiet amused smile played about Henri's lips, "Not really, It's only because he hasn't been ridden lately and he doesn't like strangers handling him. He'll calm down after a while when he becomes accustomed to everyone."

"All right, Mr. Bolkonsky, his stall is ready. I just hope he doesn't kick in its sides."

"I think I'll ride him for a while, sir, before I put him up. He needs the exercise, and for the next few days, I think it'll be safer if I take care of him myself."

Captain Harding curtly nodded his head as Henri led Vlaska away. After he put a bridle on the horse, Henri decided to dispense with the saddle. Vaulting easily onto Vlaska's back, he turned him toward an open field by the side of the stables. Vlaska broke into a mile-eating run as Henri gave him his head. Captain Harding, standing by the fence, noticed both seemed to enjoy this taste of freedom from restriction. *They compliment each other,* he thought. *They both have the same fierce wild streak kept reined in and controlled, but breaking out unexpectedly at times; and both give the impression of being extremely dangerous, needing careful handling.*

Once they had reached the middle of the long green field, Henri carefully reined Vlaska in, slowing his pace until he came to a standstill. Putting him into a slow canter, he rode to the end of the field, turned and began to practice some old Cossack tricks, including standing on the horse's back…the wind blowing through his thick blond hair.

Finally, he pulled Vlaska back to a walk returning to the stables. By the time they got there, the horse had cooled down, ready to be curried and combed. Patting Vlaska's sleek black side, Henri led him into his new stall making sure he had fresh water and hay. Captain Harding stopped him as he was about to leave, "I didn't know you knew how to ride well enough to do those tricks. Where did you learn them?"

"From my riding master…a Cossack friend of mine…my timing is still a bit off, but with practice, I'll be able to do them along with the others I learned."

"And what are they?"

Henri shrugged. "Oh, the usual, to pick up a handkerchief from the ground at a dead run, to shoot accurately from any angle, to cut the heads off sticks in the ground on both sides with a saber, to jump a fence standing on the back of one, two or three horses, to swing from a horse's back, under the neck and back into the saddle again; and so forth."

"You were taught all this?"

"Of course, as children this was all part of our training. I now keep it up just for the fun of it."

Harding gave him a long slow look. "You must have had an extremely good teacher."

"We did and a hard one." Henri grinned at the memory.

"Who do you mean by 'we'?"

"All the Bolkonsky men. You see, we were meant to go into the cavalry when we were older, so we had to know how to ride and fight from the back of a horse, saddled or not."

Thoughtfully, Harding said, "I see. All right, thank you, Mr. Bolkonsky. Tomorrow, I would like a demonstration of what else you can do."

"As you wish, sir." Henri gave him a slight bow.

Walking back to his room, Henri remained thoughtful. It had been a long time since he had tried these tricks and he hoped he could remember them. All of them involved perfect timing, coordination and a well-trained horse. He had the latter two, but only practice would give him the first. He wondered what Captain Harding had in mind. Henri was distracted from his thoughts as he heard the first bell before dinner and hurried to get changed and ready.

For Captain Harding, the demonstration the next day proved very enlightening. He realized now that Henri was an extremely advanced rider...Elite Troop quality. He decided to check into Henri's standing at the Academy. If he measured up to the standards set, he would then propose Henri for the Troop. Afterward, Harding said very little to Henri, but from then on, he paid more attention to him and was more critical of him than he was of the other men. Harding also saw to it that Henri practiced Cossack riding every day until he was absolutely perfect.

A month later, when the Companies of cavalry were being formed, Captain Harding, astride his mount, said to the assembled group, "Gentlemen, I wish to announce that the Elite Cavalry Troop will represent the Academy at the International Horse Show in London. You will be going with the rest of those who are taking part in the jumping events. I also wish to announce that I am appointing Mr. Bolkonsky to membership in The Troop. There will be a meeting of the cavalry Troop in the Drill Office immediately after this review. Companies dismissed."

Henri was surprised at this new appointment since he was still, ostensibly, a first year man, but he was also very pleased. It was an honor to be in the Elite Troop. Everyone aspired to it, but few made it for it not only depended on horsemanship, but also on scholastic standing. He quietly slipped into the Drill Office and stood at the back of the waiting men. He leaned against the wall, one leg bent, with his hands in his pockets. Relaxed, he watched the assembly curiously with no expectation of what was to happen.

"Gentlemen," Captain Harding began, "since each of you has been taking turns leading this group, it is now time to elect a person to lead the Troop during the show in London. I ask for nominations."

Silence ensued for a few minutes until Val Handly stepped forward, clearing his throat, "Sir, anticipating that Mr. Bolkonsky would be appointed a member of the Troop, the men discussed the matter while we were attending to our horses and gear. We have unanimously selected Mr. Bolkonsky to lead the Troop and I so motion."

Larry Parker immediately said, "I second the motion."

Henri pushed away from the wall. "Sir, I must decline the nomination."

Captain Harding's expression had not changed. He swung unreadable eyes toward Henri, "May I ask on what grounds you decline, Mr. Bolkonsky?"

I would hate to play poker with him! Henri thought irrelevantly, but aloud said, "On the grounds that I am the only

81

first year man in the Troop and I have been a member for less than a half hour."

"Gentlemen, you have heard Mr. Bolkonsky decline the nomination. This is open to discussion and I believe we should know the reasons why you have chosen him since his arguments are valid."

"Sir, we feel that Mr. Bolkonsky is best suited because of his horsemanship and the fact that he stands at the head of the General's Honor Roll. Also, he has shown leadership ability in the field and in the classrooms and he has won honor by his actions here at the Academy."

Steve Velp stood up, looked at Henri and added, "And, you hold the title of Prince and can steer us through the minefield of protocol. We know there will be a ball with many foreign dignitaries and diplomats, and you could keep us out of trouble!"

Everyone laughed.

"How did you find out I hold the title of Prince?"

"Val's sister sent him an article from the New York Times." Steve pulled a clipping from his wallet. "It goes like this:

Prince Henri Stephenovich Vladamir Alexander Bolkonsky has just been presented with the Distinguished Service Cross by President Harry Truman through the American Ambassador in London. The French government has already honored him with the Legion of Honour, the Croix de Guerre and the Cross of Lorraine. In addition, he holds a D.S O. and an O.B.E. from the British government. Prince Bolkonsky born in Stockholm, Sweden, is a descendant of an ancient Russian family. He is now studying at Lothian Academy in Scotland.

By now, Henri's face had become a study. He had deliberately kept all this quiet saying nothing about it to the men at the Academy, preferring they not know. He closed his eyes, thinking fast. "All right. I will try to steer you through the protocol. You're right, I do know what to do, but I do not necessarily need to lead the Troop to do that."

"Are there any more nominations?" Captain Harding asked.

"Yes," Henri said, "I would like to nominate Val Handly. I've known Val for a long time and feel he is certainly one of the best as far as leadership ability is concerned. He has shown this not only here at the Academy, but also under fire during the war." When no on immediately seconded the motion, Henri nudged the man standing next to him.

"I second the motion," he said reluctantly.

"Any more nominations?" Captain Harding asked.

"I move the nominations be closed," a voice said.

"Second."

"All in favor of Mr. Bolkonsky, please raise your hand." Everyone in the room raised his hand. "Thank you, gentlemen. I believe, Mr. Bolkonsky, you have been elected to lead the Troop." A hint of a smile touched Captain Harding's lips.

As the men drifted out of the room, Captain Harding asked Henri to stay a minute. "I have received a request from the Show Committee asking if one or more of the Cadets could provide a special show in the evenings only. I have not yet replied, but I would appreciate it if you would demonstrate the Cossack style of riding for our special contribution. I'm sorry I can't give you more time to think it over, but they want an answer before the weekend."

"If I can do it as one of the Academy men and not as an individual with unique training in Cossack horsemanship, I would be happy to do so."

"You can't remain completely anonymous, you know."

"Perhaps not, but most people who rode and fought on horseback used the same tricks—the Mongols, Arabs, Afghans, Huns and I seem to remember that the American Indians did some of the same things." Henri paused. "Could we say that it is a demonstration of an historical type of riding still used today by some warrior horsemen, rather than only Russian Cossack training?"

Harding nodded, laughing. Some of the Troop were still in the room. They came to attention at the sound and chalked it up as a red-letter day. The officer had the reputation of having the best poker face in the Academy, but Bolkonsky had stirred him to laughter.

Later, at the stable, Henri moved down the line quietly running a practiced eye over the men as they took care of their horses. Eventually, he walked into the tack room where several were looking over their equipment. He slowly circled the room checking a girth here, a stirrup there, making a quiet comment or suggestion.

Harding stood aside thinking of the way Henri had handled himself at the meeting and he watched as he toured the stable and tack room, beginning to understand why the men had picked him. Until now he had known very little about Henri and next to nothing about his background. The facts that had come out at the meeting came as a complete surprise. Henri's proud carriage; his arrogance at times; and above all, his assured manners and complete self-control, should have told Harding much sooner that Henri was accustomed to command…and had been born to wealth and privilege. As Henri came up to Captain Harding, he stopped for a minute to look back over the room. "You had better requisition some equipment, too," Harding told him.

"It's on its way. I'll pick it up in a few minutes from supply." Henri paused and searched the other man's poker face, "You do not approve their choice, do you." It was a statement rather than a question.

"Quite the contrary, I think the men picked the best person for this job," he smiled slightly.

With an imperceptible nod of his head and a slight bow, Henri left to prepare for the trip, and also to lay plans to safeguard himself while he was in London. The newspaper article had revealed his location to the world…and to his pursuers.

Chapter 9

After checking into the hotel, Henri went up to the Troop's common room and went immediately to the telephone. Impatiently, he waited for the operator to put his call through, drumming his long fingers on the table. Captain Harding, standing by the window, noticed his grim face, totally preoccupied as he ignored the comings and goings of the other men. Henri's head came up with a slight jerk, his eyes sharpening. "Henri Bolkonsky here. I want to speak with Major Robert Herring." He again waited impatiently, finally sitting on a sofa swinging one leg over the other and leaning back against the cushions. The room quieted down even though several more men came in. "Bob, how are you?" Henri's face showed relief, "No, I'm in London at the hotel."

In the now silent room, the men made no pretense of not listening. Henri, completely oblivious to them, concentrated on what he was saying and listening to the reply.

"I'm here with the Lothian Academy Cavalry Troop. We're taking part in the Horse Show. Didn't Jim tell you?...Um hum...No, I'm supposed to lead the Drill Team and am in the jumping events...Well, I'm also to do a special in Cossack type riding...Yes, alone...Don't panic, Bob, I would make a hell of a hard target to hit...Ja, you've seen it so you should know...Yes, we're to be at the ball...What is the security at the grounds?...I see. No, there are three areas that will be dangerous: the stands, the stable area and the alleyway...Right. What about the hotel? Well, that sounds a bit better...Is there a program that's being given out beforehand for those who are taking part in the show?...Are the individual names listed?...I don't know. By the way I now know how our friends found out where I was...Ja, from *The New York Times.* There was an article when I received the Distinguished Service Cross and it mentioned I was studying at the Academy in

Scotland. Damn your American papers anyway. Can't you muzzle them? How the hell did that slip by your people?"

Henri suddenly spotted the London Times lying open on the sofa next to him. Snatching it up, a broad grin spread over his face. He nearly shouted in surprised excitement, "Is Grand Duke Sergei really going to he here?...Great! Yes, yes, I know...Have Uncle Paul and the family been invited? I see." Henri's face became thoughtful. "I don't see how they can know ahead of time that I'm in the show, but they will know, or guess I'll be there as long as the show lasts...No, there's no way they can do that except with a rifle. The hotel is more dangerous...No, I don't know anyone in the British party, bit I do know most of the continental ones...Well, they may send one of them over again just for this job." A cold amused smile twitched up one corner of his lip. "You mean by that the British are less strong stomached than their counterparts or just less dedicated...No, Alexei and Jean should be relatively safe, but I will be in uniform and, therefore, easy to spot...No, I don't think so, besides I would rather they do spot me easily. I don't want the family shot up...Right, make sure you do. It would be a shame since I'm so close to home, to use one of your American phrases, to get myself killed now...Fine, I'll see you this evening...By the way, have you talked with Jim?...Right, then you're up to date on reports...I will be, don't worry. Goodbye, Bob." Henri put the telephone down thoughtfully staring into space.

Captain Harding moved away from the window over to where Henri sat. "What was that all about?" he asked.

Henri looked up at him with sardonic amusement. His veiled eyes had turned darker, nothing could be read in them. "It is very possible that an attempt on my life may be made while I'm here." He smiled slightly as he rose.

"What do you mean?" Harding demanded.

"Exactly what I said."

"Who would want to kill you?"

"The Nazis." Henri realized that Captain Harding didn't know about him. "I'm due to testify at the Nuremberg trials this summer. The Nazis do not want me to do so. I was sent to the Academy as a sort of protective confinement so that they could not get at me easily. That article blew my hiding place so that's cleared up one mystery. I've been allowed to remain because the protective coloring here is still better than anywhere else, and also to draw the fire away from my family. You will know what I mean when you meet them tonight. I called a friend of mine here to let him know I was in town and for him to expect anything."

Harding had been watching Henri with sharp eyes, as had all the men in the room. Some of them already knew the story, but there were some who did not. John Cates instinctively moved closer to Henri.

"I wish you had told me this sooner. Do you want to stay out of the show, Mr. Bolkonsky?"

Henri grinned, a strange light dancing in his eyes. Val would have recognized it, but he wasn't in the room at the moment, and Harding didn't know its significance. "No, I'll take my chances. Besides, we do have to give them a sporting chance, you know."

"Mr. Bolkonsky, it would be perfectly understandable if you wish to bow out now."

"Thank you, sir, but I do not wish to or I would not have accepted in the first place." Henri glanced at his watch. "All of you better go down for lunch. I'll join you in a minute. I want to call my family."

As the men moved out of the room, Henri picked up the telephone. He learned that Sergei and his wife, Helene, were at Knolltree, as were half the Vasilevsky clan. He also learned that his cousin, Jean, was riding in the jumping events too. It was going to be quite a contest between them for both were superb riders. He made plans with his uncle to meet him at the hotel after the ball began.

Henri was met by two young constables who dogged his steps the whole time he was at the show grounds that afternoon. They began to exasperate him, but he kept his rising impatience under control and went about his business, doing his best to ignore them. "I felt much more conspicuous with the two uniformed men constantly following me than if I were just left alone," he told Bob later. John and Val quietly stayed on either side of him while they walked back to the hotel after practice. The rest of the Troop sauntered at his back. Buses had been arranged for their transportation, but not until the following morning. Henri constantly scanned the street, cars and windows, and stood well back from the curb at the corners. He moved like a cat, tense, ready to spring in any direction at any time. His narrowed hooded eyes watched everyone and everything.

It was a relief to reach the hotel and get away from the open street. John and Val moved in front of him through the revolving doors and stood just inside to cover him. As he came through, he automatically swept the lobby with a quick glance, then tensed, riveted where he stood. Captain Harding, moving away from the desk toward them, followed his gaze.

Swiftly, Henri moved around Val and strode across the lobby to where, clearly seen through a large curtained archway behind him, a man stood at the foot of a flight of stairs leading to a small private room. He held his six-foot-three lean frame erectly in a military bearing. His deeply tanned face was clean shaven except for a small neatly clipped moustache. He wore riding clothes and, as he stood watching Henri cross the lobby toward him, lightly flicked a riding crop against his gleaming boots.

Henri knelt silently before him waiting permission to rise. Grand Duke Sergei stared down at the bent head, then slowly placing his hands on Henri's shoulders, raised him to his feet. He stood holding Henri at arms length, looking at him for a minute before taking him into his arms in the Russian greeting. "It has been a very long time, Henri Stephenovich, since I last saw you," he said, softly smiling.

"Yes, it has your Highness." Henri's blue eyes showed his pleasure at seeing Sergei again.

"How long now?"

"Several years. I was a teenager. We were at a hunt in Hungary at the time."

Sergei smiled broadly, his grey eyes sparkling. "Yes, I remember now...the boar hunt. My God, it is good to see you again."

"I'm glad you came. I heard you would be here and hoped we would meet."

"Your uncle told me where you were staying so I came right after riding. From the home movies I saw last evening, you have a good seat on a horse, but then most Bolkonskys do."

Henri smiled. "That is a great compliment coming from the best horseman in Europe."

Sergei laughed slapping Henri on his back. "Come, we must celebrate our meeting with good vodka."

"You do not mean real vodka, do you?" Henri asked in surprise and anticipation as the two men ascended the stairs and entered the private room. "I did not think one could find it with this rationing."

"That is one of the advantages of being a Grand Duke. One can always procure the real thing." Sergei led Henri by the arm up the stairs. With a flourish he produced a bottle of Krasnia Goloka, beautifully clear and chilled, and poured two small glasses. Handing one to Henri, he raised his, "Na Zdorovie."

Henri raised his glass, "Na Zdorovie." Sergei laughed at Henri's look of surprise and even more when Henri said, "My God! It is the real thing."

Sergei poured two more glasses, "It is not often you will taste this elixir. I will tell you a secret, I gave a case of it to your uncle, but do not tell him I told you. He is saving it as a surprise." He winked at Henri. "I also sent a few bottles up to your room."

He turned and was about to pour another glass when Henri held up his hand stopping him. "I'm not sure I'm allowed to drink while in uniform, your Highness. I think it might be best not to have any more right now, but later I will take advantage of the bottles in my room."

Sergei grinned. "One of the advantages of being a prince is that one can do as one pleases in or out of uniform." Catching a fleeting look that passed across Henri's face, he said more soberly, "I know, I know, that is just the sort of thinking that caused the revolution. God! How I wish the Tsar had listened to the Bolkonsky's...they would be on the throne today." Sergei tossed back the last glass, then taking Henri by the arm, led him down the stairs and toward the lobby. "Come and see Helene. Just before you came in, she disappeared to make herself more beautiful. She saw your pictures and fell in love," he said. "Ah, there she is!"

Sergei walked across the lobby calling out in a booming bass voice, "Helene, come and see my Godson, Henri Stephenovich Vladimir Alexander. He has grown into quite a man since you last saw him." He had been walking in front of Henri and now stepped aside like a magician producing a delight.

Henri bent low over her hand. Straightening up, he gazed down at her, a broad smile on his lips. Helene was also dressed in riding clothes, but since she always rode sidesaddle, looked as if she had stepped from a painting by Sargent. Her dark blue velvet habit matched her sparkling eyes. A matching hat sat at a perky angle on her elegantly coiffed blond hair. Tall for a woman, her feminine and graceful carriage was as erect as her husband's. She reached up, drawing Henri's head down to her face and kissed him on both cheeks. "You are as handsome as all the Bolkonsky men, Henri Stephenovich. I am glad to see you."

And you are more beautiful than I remembered, your Highness," he replied with a slight bow.

Sergei's booming laugh reverberated through the lobby. "I remember Helene, when Henri was madly in love with you and was like your shadow.

"I still am," Henri said softly as she held his eyes with hers.

"You have also inherited the famous Bolkonsky charm and ability to pay pretty compliments," she said.

"No, ma belle, I only tell the truth." Henri raised her hand to his lips smiling. Turning to Sergei he asked, "May I introduce the Troop to you, your Highness?"

"Of course, of course, Henri. And you have the right to call me Uncle Sergei."

With a slight bow and a smile, Henri left the Grand Duke and walked over to where Captain Harding stood with the rest of the men. They had been fascinated spectators of the scene and now waited for Henri with questions ready as he came over.

Forestalling them for the time being, he said quickly, "The Grand Duke and Grand Duchesse would like to meet all of you. Don't worry, you don't have to kneel to them, only I have to do that. Just bow and call them 'your Highness' when I introduce you." Henri was smiling and had an amused twinkle in his eye.

"This is my first chance to steer you through some protocol, and I might as well use this time for practice."

Sergei and Helene were delighted to meet the men. Henri stood by their side keeping things smooth and relaxed as he made the introductions. They spoke to each of the men individually asking about their medals and about the Academy. The men began to relax, losing some of their awe, even laughing a little.

"Are all of you to be at the ball tonight?" Helene asked sweeping the young men in her bright glance.

"Yes, your Highness," Val answered for himself and the others.

"Then it will be more fun with all you handsome young men in your uniforms." She smiled delighted. "Henri, you will be there, of course?"

"I wouldn't miss it."

"Then you must save a dance for me," she said laying her hand lightly on his arm.

"It is you who will have to save a dance for me or I will not have a chance," he answered, smiling down at her.

"I will, my young Prince. I promise."

"Do the Bolkonsky's still maintain the tradition of musicians?" Sergei broke in.

"Yes, sir, they do. Why?" Henri looked suspiciously at Sergei, guessing what was in his mind.

"Do you still dance those wild Russian folk dances?" Sergei continued, a slow thoughtful smile playing about his lips.

Henri's worst suspicions were confirmed. "Yes, but please do not do anything about it, Uncle Sergei, I beg of you."

Sergei smiled broadly. "I shall think about it," was all he would say.

Henri whirled towards Helene in desperation. "Please, ma belle, do not let him put into action what he has in mind. I beg of you. You are my last hope."

A secret amused smile played about her lips. "I shall see what I can do."

With that, Henri simply gave up and bowed. "As you wish, we are at your command."

"Now we must go. There is some reception or other and a dinner before and we must dress." Helene raised her face and Henri bent and kissed her cheek, then her hand. "Goodbye, my Prince, we will see you later."

Sergei gave Henri a parting Russian hug saying with a twinkle in his eyes, "You are allowed only one waltz with my wife, young man. Remember that or I may have to send you a challenge."

Henri bowed as they swept out with a parting wave to the assembled men. Henri, who a moment before seemed relaxed and at ease, became tense once again after the duke and duchess left the room.

When Captain Harding handed Henri's key to him, he suddenly realized the young man was an extremely good actor. Watching him while he was with the Grand Duke, no one would ever have known he expected a bullet in his back at any moment. Captain Harding was sure that the Grand Duke and his wife had no suspicion of it. Quietly, he followed Henri into the lift and up to their respective rooms.

Chapter 10

Seated at two long tables in the center of a private room, the men were finishing dinner as other diners coming in or going out of the main dining room looked curiously at them through the archway. Henri sat at one end, his back slightly toward the corner. Captain Harding noticed he had kept away from the windows and, during dinner, carefully scrutinized all those who came in or went out of the dining room.

Henri had brought the bottles of vodka and, while coffee was being served, had one of the waiters pour a small glass for each of the men.

"What exactly are Grand Duke Sergei and Helene to you? Is he a relative?" Val asked during a pause in the conversation.

Henri glanced over at him in amusement. "He is my Godfather, a distant relative of my father's, and a Vasilevsky."

"They seemed genuinely pleased to meet all of us," Val remarked, "and he is not at all what I expected of a Grand Duke."

Henri laughed. "He *was* pleased. It's been a long time since I've seen him and I was quite young, but I remember the interest he took in me and in the other young people around." His eyes took on a distant look as he cast his mind back many years. "He is one of the few men I have ever looked up to. He has the patience of Job. Much of what I know and what I am today is due to him. He was my teacher and my mentor."

Henri's voice softened and as he spoke a smile flitted about his mouth, his eyes narrowing as if he were watching a screen. "God, he has patience. He always had time to answer my questions and to show me what I must do. I followed him around like a puppy dog...always on his heels. He never became impatient or angry as most others would have. It seemed as if he went out of his way to include me, to teach me, to help me.

"When I was ten-years-old, we were in Hungary on a boar hunt, my first. I heard the baying of the hounds, and the crash as the huge beast tore through the underbrush out into the open…a huge monster, hideous and vicious. His tusks, a dull ivory, razor sharp, could disembowel a horse in seconds. God help the man who is unhorsed, for he will be dead before anyone can save him. The boar stood frozen for a minute, magnificent in his ugliness, looking quickly around before he started his maddened rush. Then he came with the speed of a Spanish fighting bull and equally as savage.

"He came at me with all the black hatred of the devil gleaming in his little eyes. Thank God my horse was well trained and Uncle Sergei was nearby; otherwise, I would not be here today. The boar hit my lance sending a shock through my body that almost unseated me. It kept charging in blind fury, its eyes red with rage. I leaned on my lance, terrified, thinking the beast would never give up. Sergei saw what was happening and rode over fast, shouting encouragement and advice. Finally, after what seemed a millennium, the beast heeled over and died. I will never forget the proud look in Sergei's eyes or the smile on his face. I did not dare let him see that I was sick with exhaustion.

"That night, everyone was happy and we all danced and sang into the small hours of the morning. One of the grooms taught me several of the Hungarian dances. I had a little dark eyed, dark haired girl to dance with all night. I was eleven and she was about nine and had long beautiful braids falling down her back.

"The skies were clear and I felt as if I could almost reach up, touch the stars and hold them in my hands. The plains stretched as far as I could see and beyond. It was a good year; the harvest had been good; the people were well fed; there was laughter to be heard; and the hunt had gone well. I can still smell the boars roasting over the fires, the sound of music as the peasants sang and danced and the colors of their costumes as they flashed by, lighted by the fires."

Henri's voice, now somber, continued, "It was a happy time. I never thought that four years later my family would be dead; that the clear skies I looked up to that night would be filled with bombers carrying death; the endless plains would be covered by an endless stream of tanks and men; the laughter would be turned to screams; nor the smell of roasting boar would be replaced by the smell of burning human flesh; that the peasants and the children would starve and die by the thousands; or that the only music would be the marching of jackboots over the bones of the dead.

"And now the same horrors which we fought to end are beginning all over again. The secret night arrests; the imprisonment without trial; the total disappearance of human beings from the face of the earth; the labor camps and the tortures, along with the crushing of the human will." Henri's voice had dropped to a harsh whisper then rose in a cynical parody of an age-old toast, "Hitler is dead; long live Stalin."

Throwing back his head, he drank the vodka down in one gulp, crushing the glass in his hand. His eyes, which had been far away as if he hadn't been in the room, suddenly returned. Scanning the faces of the spellbound men, he rose abruptly. "Sorry, I didn't mean to climb on my soapbox." He glanced at his watch. "It's about time we dressed."

Captain Harding rose with him and caught his arm as he was about to leave. Picking up a linen serviette, he silently wrapped it around Henri's bleeding hand.

"Thank you," Henri murmured with a twisted smile and went up to his room to dress for the ball.

The room was a mass of movement, talk and laughter The glittering array of multihued gowns and jewels worn by the feminine guests vied with the men in their dress uniforms, gleaming medals and red sashes across their chests. One could feel the electric excitement and gaiety flowing in waves as the guests, for a few hours, forgot the rationing and the queues.

The ballroom was made to seem twice as long by the wall of mirrors behind the orchestra's raised dais. Little gold stands in front of wine red cushioned chairs stood with their sheets of music waiting for the musicians to arrive. By the time Henri and the Troop entered the room, a number of guests were already seated around the small gold colored tables encircling the highly polished floor. Bob Herring stood close to the receiving line waiting for them. As Henri and Captain Harding left the line, Bob approached them. "Good evening, Henri, how are things going?"

"Fine. The practice went well this afternoon, but I do wish you would call off those two watchdogs you put on my tail. They make me more conspicuous than if they were not around."

"They are just a temporary measure until I can get others. Tomorrow, I will have two plainclothesmen instead. They'll be dressed in riding clothes and will stay at a distance. Will that be better?"

"Much better, thanks." Sweeping his eyes over the crowd, he said with an amused look in his eyes, "Quite a group here tonight."

"Yes, isn't there. It looks as if all London has turned out."

"More like London, Paris, Rome and assorted others." A quirk started to tug at the corners of Henri's mouth as his eyes continued to sweep over the room.

Bob looked at him curiously, "What is amusing you so?"

"The Russian contingent. They seem to be keeping the dance floor between them like a no man's land between two battling armies. The Vasilevsky and the Bolkonskys on one side all looking gay, having a jolly good time and flouting it, while our good comrades, on the opposite side, sit looking determined not to have a good time and casting sour, affronted glances in their direction."

Bob grinned. "I wish you could have seen Ordonov's face when he first walked in. I wasn't sure if he was going to stay or leave."

"I can imagine," Henri said with a short laugh and a half smile. "Oh! Bob, let me introduce you to Captain Harding. This is Major Robert Herring, the friend I telephoned this morning." Henri stepped back slightly.

"I gathered as much. Good evening major," Harding said holding out his hand.

"Captain." Bob bowed slightly and shook hands. Turning back to Henri, his face becoming serious, he said, "We have you well covered and none of our friends have shown up yet. There will always be two of our men very close to you so do not worry and do not get edgy."

"Right. I'm not too worried about someone coming at me with a knife. I can dodge a blade, but not a bullet."

"Henri!" a voice rang out. He turned to see Vasili coming toward him across the empty expanse of the ballroom floor. With a quick nod of his head to Bob and the captain, Henri went to meet him. They greeted each other enthusiastically, for they had been friends from childhood. Vasili, a little shorter and stockier than Henri had light brown hair and dark brown eyes. "My God! Where did you spring from and what are you doing in that uniform?"

"I've been in Scotland the past few months studying hard at an academy there. It's good to see you again. How is the family? Are they here tonight?"

Vasili, who would not be sidetracked, persisted. "Don't tell me you are going to keep to the Bolkonsky military tradition here in this country?" He shook his head smiling then holding Henri at arms length. "Well, you are looking good. It must suit you."

At this moment, Andrew walked across to the two young men. Older by several years and a little more restrained than they, he too greeted Henri with enthusiasm, his grey eyes dancing. He stood half a head shorter than Henri, but was well built, muscular, and Henri noticed with amusement that, judging from the stares of the women as Andrew had crossed the room, he was still a lady killer.

Henri broke away from his two friends and went to meet Natasha when he saw her walking toward them. Her emerald green gown matched her beautiful green eyes rimmed by long dark sweeping eyelashes. Titian hair was caught up at the back of her small elegant head cascading from there down her back in long ringlets. No makeup marred her fair skin except for a very pale touch of lipstick. Her smile was brilliant as she held out a small delicate hand. Henri bent low over her hand and kissed her on both cheeks. "Natasha, you're looking ravishing tonight as usual. How are you?"

"Henri, my love, be careful or I may take you seriously," she teased him. Her eyes danced with pleasure for Henri and she had been childhood sweethearts and they had retained a closeness over the years. Placing her hand lightly on his arm, she asked in mock despair, "Why have you not come to visit us? You said you would and I have told all my beautiful friends you were coming. I have even shown them the picture of you I keep on the mantle in my bedroom. Their hearts will be broken if you do not."

When Henri was with the Vasilevskys as well as other Russian groups, a latch seemed to be released. Suddenly, he became light-hearted, automatically matching his mood with theirs. Now he placed his hand over his heart in mock contriteness. "I am truly sorry, Natasha, but I have been extremely busy and just not able to make it, but I will come, I promise."

"When? I am going to have to pin you down to a date. It is almost impossible to get hold of you and you never answered my letters." Natasha frowned severely.

Again I apologize, my love. I've been in Scotland. I promise I will answer all your letters promptly in the future. I'm afraid though, I will not be able to visit until sometime in the fall."

"But why, Henri? That's too long away. Come this summer and spend a month with us." Natasha was no longer teasing, but had become quite serious.

"I'd love to, ma belle, but I must go to the Continent this summer so this fall will be the earliest."

"All right then, my name day is in October. You must come for my party and stay with us," she said quickly.

"I'll try my best, ma cherie." He remained evasive.

"Promise?" She cocked her head to one side, looking up at him through her long beautiful lashes.

"I will promise to try my best, but at this point I cannot promise definitely." Henri smiled down at her. "You are hard to resist, my love," he added softly.

Shaking her head, she dropped her eyes and said with a despairing sigh, "You are perfectly terrible, *mon cher*."

Henri grinned at her and gave her a light kiss on the cheek. By this time, Captain Harding and the rest of the men had formed a loose group behind Henri. Turning he said, "Now let me introduce you to some of my friends." Vasili, Andrew and Natasha gaily talked for a short time while Henri watched quietly.

Then Natasha beckoned to him, "Mama wants to see you, Henri, and has been waiting impatiently." She took him by the arm, leading him to where her mother was seated. As Henri bent low and kissed her outstretched hand, he had to admire this lovely gracious woman. He noticed that she wore a severely black slightly flared gown which showed off her still beautiful figure to restrained perfection. Inevitable, the diamond and emerald necklace, given her by the Grand Duke Michael, lay around her slim neck.

. Princess Marie bent her regal white head slightly, smiling up at him. She had always liked and approved of Henri and had hoped that one day he and her daughter would marry. But as they grew older, they had become more like brother and sister, and Marie realized that her fond hope for this marriage might never be. Marie had small, delicate bones and beautiful emerald green eyes which had been famous in her day. She had been known as the most beautiful and bewitching of the crown jewels. "Good evening Henri Stephenovich, it is good to see you again. We have been looking forward to a visit from you."

"I am sorry, your Highness, but it has been impossible. Perhaps later on in the fall." Henri's eyes and smile were gentle as he looked down at her.

"What are you doing now, my dear?"

"At the moment, I'm studying at the Lothian Military Academy."

"Who are the handsome young men with you tonight?" she asked.

"They are the Academy Cavalry Troop which will be in the show tomorrow." Looking over at them, he had to admit they did look exceedingly well in their dark blue tails, a red stripe down each trouser leg, white shirts and medals.

"Ah! So I was right and it was you they were speaking of in the paper today," she said. "I should like to meet them. They all look so handsome in their uniforms."

Henri didn't have time to ask her what she meant or what paper she was talking about, as she had already placed her hand lightly on his arm. At the moment, all he could do was bow and say, "As you wish," and lead her to where the men were standing. As he came toward them, they responded to his silent signal to form up and guessed correctly they were to meet yet another royal personage and they immediately stood at attention.

"Henri," Princess Marie said with some asperity, "Please have your men stand at ease. I am not reviewing the Troops and I wish to meet them informally."

A secret smile played about Henri's mouth, amusement lighting his eyes. "Yes, your Highness. As you were, men." He introduced each of them to the Princess and each of them bowed and kissed her extended hand. Glancing over at Vasili, a wide grin spread over his face. They both had the same thought. The Princess, no matter what she said, was still regally reviewing the Troops, albeit graciously.

After Henri led Princess Marie back to her seat, Paul came to rescue him and take him to where the family sat. He again signaled the men to follow as he moved beside his uncle. His cousins greeted him enthusiastically with loud gay shouts, laughter, and hugs. After this wild exuberance, Henri introduced the men a little more sedately to the family. "And this is my cousin Carlotta. You'll remember that I told you about her," he said unable to keep back a smile. Carlotta proceeded to charm all of them. For the rest of the evening, she not once lacked dancing partners, which amused Henri, her brother Jean, and Alexei.

Helene beckoned Henri to come to her table where she was surrounded by her usual court. As he approached, she made room next to her on the little sofa. "Henri Stephenovich come sit here by me," she said as he bent over her hand.

"Helene, you are going to make many enemies for me tonight. When may I have my first waltz with you?" He gingerly sat on the edge of the sofa so as not to crush Helene's bouffant white satin gown. She had artistically arranged it to show the white seed pearls that were scattered over her skirt.

She made a great show of consulting an imaginary card dangling from her wrist, finally saying in her best operetta voice, "I am afraid, mon amour, not until after supper can I possibly fit you in."

"My heart will be broken if I cannot hold you in my arms at least once this evening, ma belle, and you did promise to save me one dance." Henri managed to look both hopeful and heartbroken at the same time.

"And I will keep my promise. Let me see, you may be number seventy-one." With a flourish, she wrote his name in the air and, holding the imaginary card for him, said gaily, "There now I have written your name, see?"

Henri grabbed her hand and kissed it passionately. They both burst out laughing just as Sergei came up. "Ah! There you are Henri. I should have known you would be here with Helene. I see I will have to keep my eye on both of you from now on."

Henri rose and bowed, "Your vodka was appreciated by all, Uncle Sergei. Thank you for sending the bottles to my room."

"Did the boys really like it?" he asked smiling broadly.

"Very much, sir."

"Good, then I will send more over to you tomorrow." Glancing around, he continued, "This is quite a brilliant gathering tonight, don't you think?"

"That it is, sir." Henri looked at him out of the corner of his eye and with a smile twitching at the corners of his mouth asked, "What do you think of our comrades across the way?"

Sergei's answer was drowned by the fanfare announcing the arrival of the Lord Mayor and his Lady, which was just as well, Henri thought, as Sergei was about to make some rude comment. The first strains of a waltz floated through the ballroom and Sergei led Helene onto the floor, while Henri drifted back to his family.

While he talked with his many friends or danced, Henri remained alert, his eyes constantly roving over the room. He spotted several of Bob's men dressed as waiters and knew others were scattered throughout the crowd. No one, even those who knew Henri well were aware of his tense vigilance.

Just before midnight Sergei came over to the family group and touched Henri's arm. "It is about time for all of you to go and change. Will you round up Alexei, Jean, Carlota and the others?"

"What are you talking about?" Henri asked suspiciously.

"You are to dance tonight. Andrew, Natasha, Olga, Xenia, Julia and Vasili will be joining you."

"But we don't have our costumes here, Uncle Sergei, and we certainly can't dance in these clothes."

"Ah! But Paul brought your costumes and they are waiting for you in the men's room." Sergei smiled confidently.

"But the orchestra doesn't know..." Henri began to protest.

Sergei broke in, "Oh! But they do. The whole thing has been arranged and the Lord Mayor is looking forward to seeing all of you dance."

Henri didn't mind dancing for their small circle of friends but to do so in front of such a large gathering of complete strangers filled him with horror. His face was a study as he desperately searched for a way out of it, but every objection he raised, Sergei countered and finally he had to give in.

The lights dimmed in the supper room and the noise of the crowd died at the opening strains of the first dance. Paul tapped out the rhythms with his foot, wishing he were out there dancing too. Even the Russian Embassy group seemed to enjoy it, tapping and clapping to the music.

When it was time for their finale "The Knife Dance," Paul stepped up to the orchestra and took over an accordion starting the first bars of the North Caucasian melody and a hush fell over the audience.

Carlotta stepped forward holding Alexei's arm, while outrageously flirting over her shoulder with Henri, who followed closely behind...and the dance began, Alexei becoming more and more annoyed until he turned and challenged Henri to a duel. Gleaming knives appeared in their hands and the two began to circle. At this moment, Jean leaped in, parting them with an imperious upward sweep of his arm and taking a knife from his belt, flipped it point first into the floor between the two antagonists.

The audience gasped...a momentary silence...and a shot exploded!

Screams rang out as Henri whirled to see Jean clutch his shoulder and stagger back against Paul. Alexei started toward Jean, but Henri called to Alexei to follow him as in five great strides, he crossed the dance floor after the shooter who headed for an open door into the lobby. Leaping to the center of a table which stood in his way, Henri launched himself onto the man's back bringing him down. In a blind rage, Henri put his hands around the man's throat and began to choke him.

102

Sergei and Alexei had both caught up with Henri and with the aid of Captain Harding and Val, managed to loosen his grip. It took the four of them to hold him off. Sergei kept repeating, "Jean is all right, Henri. It's just a shoulder wound. Let the security guards handle it now."

The rage ebbed out of Henri. He relaxed his tense body and turned to look for Jean. The Russian doctor was bending over his cousin while Paul and Alicia stood by Jean's chair. With long strides, Henri was beside them, anger still flashing in his eyes. "How is Jean, doctor?"

"He'll be all right. The bullet grazed his shoulder, but did no damage. I'm just going to stop the bleeding and bandage it, and then I suggest you take him to hospital for further treatment."

"Thank you." Henri glanced at Paul who nodded.

"That bullet was meant for you," Paul stated.

"I know and the stupid idiot had to choose the wrong target," Henri said between clenched teeth.

"I'm glad it was me and not you, Henri." Jean spoke for the first time, opening his eyes to grin up at him. "It's not that bad and besides you've had a rough enough time of it."

"You are the last person I wanted see get hurt." Henri's voice was still angry. "If he had known his business, he would never have made that mistake."

The doctor finished and now looked from one to the other, a small smile flickering about his mouth. "I've heard about your quick reactions and co-ordination. I must admit I had not expected it to be so dramatically demonstrated. I have also heard that your family closes ranks quickly when attacked, but I did not really believe it until now."

Henri pivoted until he was directly facing the doctor, his eyes suddenly watchful. "Apparently, you have heard a great deal about us, which I find rather strange."

"Not so strange since my mother comes from the land the Bolkonskys used to own. I know a lot about your family and most of its members. You are still quite famous in those parts of Russia," the doctor said with a slightly amused smile.

Henri's face remained guarded. "I see. I thought I caught the trace of an accent when you spoke, but I wasn't sure."

The doctor smiled and bowed. "Your son will need to be taken to hospital, Mr. Bolkonsky," he said looking at Paul, "but I think he will be all right now."

"Thank you very much for your help, doctor. We all appreciate it." Paul bowed slightly and the doctor turned away going back to his own group. Paul and Henri helped Jean to his feet and led him from the room as the family closed in behind them.

Chapter 11

Henri saddled his horse, and glanced up the line at the men, waiting, ready to mount and move out. Tethering his horse, he was about to make a last minute inspection when Alexei approached him, "Henri, do you know where Captain Harding is?"

"No, but what are you doing here? I thought you were in the box. How is Jean by the way?"

"He's fine and thoroughly enjoying all the attention which Mother is lavishing on him. You know how she is." Alexei laughed. "Father sent me to ask the Captain if he would like to watch the Musical Ride with us."

"Good idea. Will Jean be able to ride in the jumping events?"

"The doctor said he would be all right; so he's planning on it."

"Great. It's going to be fun riding against him." Henri looked up nodding his head. "Captain Harding has just come around the corner."

"Right. I'll see you later." Alexei bowed to Captain Harding. "With my father's compliments, would you join us in the box for the rest of the evening, sir?"

"Thank you, I would like that very much. I haven't seen the Team except from the railing."

"It's much better from where we are, sir; one has a good view of the patterns."

As the two men moved off, Henri started up the line. He was in a gay mood, a smile twitching up the corners of his mouth and his eyes sparkling. Softly, he sang to himself,

> The Gypsy rover came over the hill
> He came through the valley so shady
> He whistled and he sang
> And he won the heart of a lady.

105

Henri whistled the next phrase of the song as his quick eyes checked men, gear and horses. Reaching out to straighten a chain as he passed, he continued singing softly to himself,

> She left her father's castle gate
> She left her own fond lover.
> She left her servants and her state
> To follow her Gypsy lover.

Picking up a brush, he ran it quickly over a hind quarter,

> Her father saddled up his fastest speed
> Roamed the valleys all over
> Sought his daughter at great speed
> And the whistling Gypsy Rover.

Returning to his own horse, he mounted and, turning sideways, called out, "Mount up." The men leaped to obey for they too were in a good mood taking their cue from Henri. A smile lightened up his face as he said with a laugh in his voice, "If any of you slip up tonight, I will cheerfully strangle the lot of you. The men grinned back. "Right. Now fall in and form up." He waited until all the men were lined up by twos, and then gave the signal to move out.

Leading them, he sat his horse casually, holding the reins loosely in one hand, with the other hooked into his belt. He was still singing as they rode toward the ring,

> He came at last to a mansion fine
> Bound by the river Plaidy
> And there was music and there was wine
> For the Gypsy and his lady.

The announcer's voice brought them to full attention. "Ladies and Gentlemen, we are pleased to present the Lothian Academy Precision Riding Team. The maneuvers you will see tonight were originally developed as cavalry exercises enabling a troop to move in any direction quickly and in unison. The figures are formed by individual horses and riders, by twos, fours and eights, either at a trot or canter."

Looking back for the last time, Henri checked the team. As the first strains of the "Radetsky March" rang out, he straightened in his saddle, excitement suddenly mounting within him. Unconsciously, his arrogant carriage became evident as he started his horse forward through the gate into the ring, the Troop following him.

Paul smiled as they appeared, remembering the reviews before the Tsar many years ago and of the many generations of Bolkonskys who had led their troops on parade down the Nevsky Prospeckt. His nephew had the same air about him as they all had...the rapier straight back; the arrogant cant to the head; the perfectly blank face; the heavy lidded Asian eyes partly hooded. All these were characteristic, and Henri was no exception.

The team moved at a fast trot splitting into two columns riding on either side of the ring before beginning their figures. Henri was aware of the eyes watching him: his family's; Grand Duke Sergei and Helene; Vasili, Natasha, Andrew; Princess Marie; as well as those from the other side of the Russian fence. As he passed the two boxes where his family, Sergei and Helene sat, he had difficulty keeping his face blank. He wanted to break into a grin or burst into laughter. His mood was one of bubbling champagne in spite of the danger that lurked in the hidden shadows.

As they finished and rode smartly out of the ring, Henri began to sing to himself again,

> He is no Gypsy my father she said
> But Lord of these lands all over
> And I will stay 'till my dying day
> With my whistling Gypsy rover.

Once back in the stable area, Henri sat his horse watching as the men rode by to their places. Before giving the order to dismount, he smiled. "Thank you Gentlemen, everything went perfectly tonight with no mistakes. I think this calls for breaking out some of Sergei's vodka after the show." Seeing the looks on the men's faces, he laughed, gave the order to dismount and dropped easily off his horse.

Henri sat with two other Academy men waiting for the decision of the Team Event. Big grins spread over their faces when they learned they were in the lead. Now they would begin counting the points until the end of the week when the Team with the highest score would take the big silver trophy home. Henri rode back to the stable area to change for his special event. He had time between the two events, as the Hackney ponies would be in the ring for a while. Leisurely, he changed into a white silk Russian blouse, black sash, black trousers and boots and slipped a short riding crop around his wrist. He saddled Vlaska and reached the ring in time to hear the announcement. "Taught by the Cossacks to ride as a child, we are privileged to present, from the Lothian Academy, his Highness Prince Henri Stephenovich Vladimir Alexander Bolkonsky."

Henri rode into the ring to the music of "Cossack Patrol" and at this point wished he had never agreed to do this. The announcement embarrassed him, but he was in it now and had to make the best of it. After completing a few tricks picking up a saber from his saddle and showing a bow at various targets, he dropped off Vlaska and sent him out of the ring.

He signaled Val and Chris to come into the ring, bringing the three horses he was to use in the next part of his demonstration. Henri grabbed the mane of one of the horses and vaulted onto its bare back, reining it into a rearing stop.

Standing on its back, he guided the horse around the ring taking one jump and then another. As they reached the third, a second horse came along side where Henri placed one foot on his back and with one foot on the first horse and one foot on the other, He took the next jump and signaled for a third horse to join him. He picked up this horse as he had the second and when the band broke into "Mtschiza Trojha," he gathered the three pairs of reins in one hand, cracking a whip over the troika's heads. This time, he took two jumps on one side and two on the other side of the ring.

The spectators first held their breaths and then broke into thunderous applause. Now, they were treated to a most amazing demonstration. Henri began dropping off one horse between that one and the next and then leaping up on the bare back of the next horse. Then he vaulted over each horse in turn, landing on his feet on the back of the last horse. The crowd went wild.

Henri's family were on their feet with Paul and Sergei gripping the railing in front of them until their knuckles turned white. Sergei muttered under his breath, "Wait until I get my hands on him. I'll throttle him unless he kills himself first! Alexei and Jean were in the alley between the ring and the audience, ready to vault into the ring the instant Henri made a mistake.

Cracking the whip with a flourish, Henri headed the three horses into the jumps for the last time. He brought the troika skidding around and up the center of the ring. The gates swung open as he sent the horses out of the ring pulling them up short just outside the gates. Looking back, he saw the stands in pandemonium and, above all, he saw the Red Army men on their feet clapping and yelling, "Bravo!" Quietly, he dropped off the horse he was standing on, an irrepressible smile on his face, then quietly, he went back to change for the Individual Jumpers Event.

When Henri had changed into his regular uniform for the Jumping Event, Captain Harding approached him with a man, whom Henri did not recognize.

"Mr. Bolkonsky, this is Mr. Mason, Assistant Coordinator of the show. You asked to see him, I understand."

"Yes. It is about the announcement that was made tonight. I did not give permission to use my title and full name. I do not wish to have it used in the future."

"I understand, your Highness, but please hear me out. I looked for you after practice today to ask permission, but could not find you. I apologize." He bowed slightly as he said the last words and continued, "My real name is Masurian. I am Russian, also, though not of the nobility. I am of Zaporogian Cossack stock. My father fought with the Whites under General Deniken in the Ukraine during the Civil War and eventually escaped to Manchuria, then China, America and finally to Britain.

"There is out there a block of seats taken by members of the Red Army who are here in London. I just wanted them to know that a member of the nobility could do anything they can do and do it better."

A slow smile spread across Henri's face as he listened to this explanation. For a minute, he stood looking at the earnest face of Mr. Mason/Masurian, before the laugh that began deep within him finally bubbled over into his eyes and out. He placed both his hands on Mason's shoulders and said, "All right, just this once. I accept your apology; but remember, no other night of the week can you use it. All right?"

Mason smiled and nodded his head. "Thank you, your Highness. You will never know how much pleasure this has given my father and me. He and my mother came here especially tonight after I told them about you. I remember watching my father do some of the tricks you do but neither of us has seen real Cossack riding for a long time. Tonight was a very special one for all of us."

He and Henri understood each other well. There was an unholy gleam in Henri's eyes. "Good. We did make them sit up and take notice, didn't we?" With a parting bow, Henri mounted his horse for the Jumping Event. He was whistling softly to himself as he rode toward the ring.

Again, the three Academy men sat on their horses outside the ring listening to the results. Henri relaxed with one leg crossed over the saddle leaning his elbow on his knee. Pantelon had been his usual wild self, a big bay with white stockings and powerful hindquarters, standing sixteen and a half hands, and with a mouth like iron. It took all of Henri's strength to hold him in. Pantelon wanted to gallop into the jumps, but would crash them if he was allowed. Henri had to hold him back; forcing him to walk; releasing him at the last moment; only then would he take anything and everything in his path. It was not so bad, except Pantelon also had a habit of rearing and screaming, fighting the reins all the way as he went.

Over the loudspeaker came the announcement. "Two horses have tied for first place. There will be a jump off. Number Two, Blackbird, ridden by Jean Bolkonsky and Number Seven, Pantelon, ridden by Henri Bolkonsky."

"Unless something happens, Jean is going to be my greatest rival for the cup," Henri said, as he put his foot back into the stirrup.

"Good luck," Val called as Henri moved off.

"The jumps have been raised to five foot nine and six feet. The course will be the same," the disembodied voice announced.

Blackbird went first, seeming to effortlessly sail over the jumps. Henri, watching from his vantage point just behind the gates, nodded his head in approval, admiring the beautiful horse and Jean's skill as a rider. As Blackbird finished, the announcer reported, "Two faults for Number Two. Time is 118.4 seconds."

Henri gathered the reins in and felt Pantelon quiver under him. The gates were open and the horse reared, letting out his first scream as he pulled against the bit and reins. The course was a twisting one with twelve jumps in all. As Pantelon finished the last jump, the announcer said, "Clean round for Number Seven. Time 120.2 seconds."

Henri reached out and patted the horse's neck. "Good boy, Pantelon, you won this round. Just keep it up for the rest of the week."

As Henri came around the corner, he spotted Igor and Pyotr waiting for him, their faces like thunder and he knew he was in for trouble. He really expected Sergei and his uncle to be waiting for him, not these two. He didn't change the expression on his face as he rode up to them, pretending he didn't notice anything wrong, continuing to laugh and joke with Val and Chris who were riding next to him.

Pyotr caught the reins as Henri slid down from the saddle to face a scowling Igor. Igor drew himself up to his full six foot six glaring down at Henri. Biting each word, he snapped, "Just exactly what did you think you were doing out there tonight, your Highness? Do you realize how easily you could have killed yourself and neither Pyotr nor I could have saved you?"

"You were always reckless, even as a child, but tonight you exceeded yourself! Very few, if any, Cossacks with any brains at all would have attempted those tricks!" Pyotr growled, cutting in on Igor.

The two brothers stood side by side and, both being the same height, dwarfed Henri's slim six foot three frame. Both men had basso profundo voices that, when angry, sounded like thunder rumbling in the distance. They could be heard all the way down the aisle. The Troop began to gather to listen. None of them were quite sure what the brothers were talking about, but guessed it had something to do with the unrehearsed parts of the special riding event.

"Neither Pyotr nor I ever taught you those tricks and if I ever lay my hands on the one who did, I will strangle him!"

"Since he is about ninety now, I doubt he would mind."

"The trouble is you were not disciplined enough as a child! If your father were here, he would give you a sound thrashing for what you did out there tonight! You put his direct line in jeopardy."

Henri threw back his head and laughed. Then he placed one hand on Igor's shoulder and the other on Pyotr's and said more soberly, "I had a reason for doing what I did tonight and I accomplished what I set out to do, but I promise, on my word of honor, I will not do those particular tricks again. I know it was reckless and foolish but..." he shrugged his shoulders. "Now will you two stop worrying about me and forgive me?" He looked from one scowling face to the other, his eyes dancing in merriment, a half smile on his lips.

Igor and Pyotr began to soften, finally nodding their heads. "But do not ever let me catch you even thinking of doing them again! You are my master, but I will take a whip to you." Igor smiled shaking his head in despair.

Henri slapped their backs and turned to face another storm. Paul, Sergei and the family had been standing listening. Henri had spotted them as they came up. Captain Harding was with them and, much to Henri's surprise he noticed General Dayton, Colonel Grey and Doctor White with them.

"Young man, I hope you mean what you told Igor and Pyotr. If you ever dare to try those tricks again, I will personally beat the bloody hell out of you!" Paul got in, before Sergei could say anything. "Of all the stupid, reckless, harebrained things to pull, this took the cake!"

"You nearly gave your Aunt a heart attack, and Maria and Carlotta would not even watch they were so afraid, to say nothing of Helene! Your thoughtless tempting of death had us all sick with fear!" Sergei's eyes were flashing. "There are times when I do not think you have the sense of a newborn babe."

Henri was trying to look contrite, but not succeeding very well. "Uncle Paul, Uncle Sergei, I think you both know why I did it, so I will not go into long explanations. I will admit it was foolish and very dangerous, but deep down you have to admit that it did your hearts good to see the sons of your enemies cheering one of Russian nobility. I know it is not a good reason and certainly not one to risk one's neck for, but that is the way it is. Henri cocked his head to one side smiling, his mischievous eyes dancing.

Paul began to soften, but his face and eyes remained angry. He glared at Henri for a full minute before saying, "In all honesty, it did do my heart good, but that still does not excuse you. It doesn't surprise me that you know those tricks. You were always headstrong and willful, even as a child."

"You seem to love to live as close to danger as possible, young man," Sergei cut in. "Why, I don't know. Your heedless act scared everyone out of their wits tonight. If you want to play those dangerous games, then do so, but not in front of those who care for you."

Paul placed both hands on Henri's shoulders, a smile twitching up the corners of his mouth, but his eyes serious. "All right, you are forgiven, but do not, under any circumstances, do it again."

"I promise, Uncle Paul."

Suddenly, the aisle became a hive of activity with people laughing and talking at the same time, interspersed with shouts and hugs as other old friends arrived. Visitors outside of this select group would be excused if they thought they had stepped into a foreign country for conversations in French, German, Russian, Italian and Spanish could be heard above the English as well as Polish, Hungarian and Swedish.

Henri moved in and out of the crowd stopping here or there to talk in whatever language was being spoken at the time. He seemed to be everywhere a once, his gaiety infecting everyone around him. Jean and Alexei were just as boisterous as were all the younger people. None of the Academy men had ever seen Henri in this completely relaxed outgoing mood but this was not the only time he amazed them and it would not be the last.

Slowly, the aisle cleared as the visitors left to go to parties or home to their beds. All that were left were Henri's immediate family. The members of the Troop made last minute checks of the horses before leaving for the night. Henri was talking with his family when a low quiet voice behind him said, "Henri Stephenovich, you did some magnificent riding tonight."

Henri whirled around, disbelief showing on his face. He stood rooted to the ground until the shock wore off, then he leaped, throwing his arms around a tall quiet serious faced man. It was several minutes before they stood at arms length looking at each other, "Ladislaus! I cannot believe it! You are alive!" Henri finally said when he found his voice again.

"Yes, I am and I am glad to see that you are too." Ladislaus' face lit in a gay smile as he looked at Henri.

"I went back to find you but the old one would not tell me where you were." Henri still gripped his arms as if afraid if he let go Ladislaus would disappear.

"I told her to tell you that. It would have been too dangerous for you to have found me. Besides the Germans were breathing down your neck and you were only one step ahead of them."

"Then you *were* in the mountains," Henri said softly, as if remembering a cryptic word and discovering its meaning long after. "I could have smuggled you out."

"I know you would have tried, but you would have been caught in the process…besides, I had to remain. I could not have left then. You know that, my friend."

Henri simply nodded his head, then suddenly seeing two other men standing behind his friend, greeted them enthusiastically, "Jan! Yurick! My God! It is good to see you."

The two men greeted Henri with equal enthusiasm. It was obvious to those watching that these four had known each other for a very long time. Paul gathered from their conversation they came out of the war years, and by their names, they had known each other in Hungary. He would have loved to have known the story behind this friendship. It was obvious to anyone observing them that Henri was deeply moved to see them again.

"Come have dinner with me and we can talk. I want to catch up on your lives," Herri said. "I have a thousand and one questions."

"We must leave for Switzerland tonight, Henri." There was real sadness in Ladislaus' grey eyes as he spoke. "I wish we could."

"How are Mary and my godson?" Henri asked.

"They're fine and we have a daughter now, too," he replied smiling. "You must see her. She looks just like her mother."

"Congratulations," Henri said. "When will you be back here?"

"I have no idea. There is still so much work to be done and it is far more difficult now in these days." Ladislaus' face was serious again and his eyes held a deep sadness which was never very far from the surface.

"I see," Henri said quietly, watching his friend intently. "All right, I will be in Germany this summer at the end of June, the first part of July. I will come to Switzerland afterward. Will you be there then?"

At this, Ladislaus smiled. "Yes, and we have just moved into a large house in the country and have lots of room, so you can stay with us."

"Great. Then tell Mary to expect me about the middle of July."

The two men parted almost silently. Henri held Ladislaus, gripping his shoulder. "Take care. If you ever need me, you know how to get in touch. I will come."

Ladilaus nodded his head, turned quickly on his heel and walked away. Henri parted with Jan and Yuric the same way, watching them leave with a pensive look in his eyes.

"Mr. Bolkonsky, will you look at Major's leg. I think there is something wrong with it," Jimmy broke in on his thoughts.

With a sigh, Henri turned, coming back from wherever he had been, to the aisle, the horse and the Troop. His exuberance gone, he had returned to his quiet withdrawn self.

Chapter 12

Paul invited the Troop, including General Dayton, Colonel Grey, Doctor White and Captain Harding, to have dinner with the family. He took them to an old Russian restaurant, near the West End, run by two old friends of his. Located in the basement of a building in the middle of the block, its unpretentious entrance hid a spacious room where Ivan and his wife, Melushka, did their own cooking. Their three daughters and two sons waited on tables. Known to have the best Russian food in London it was always crowded.

An oval Zakuska table stood near the door, always beautifully decorated and constantly replenished with a variety of foods, which changed from night to night. In these post war days, no one knew where Ivan found the food. It remained a deep mystery, but night after night the table offered up its ever-changing delicacies. This evening, they consisted of a sturgeon in aspic with carrot daises; two pots of caviar, one red and one black; a chicken based *Salat Olivier*; pate with a wreath of turnip rosebuds; pickled herring encircled by a necklace of onion rings; three kinds of bread with unsalted butter lilies, a bowl of fresh fruits; pickles; pickled mushrooms and an assortment of vodkas.

A small orchestra played Russian, Polish and Hungarian folk music, the guests providing the singing and dancing. Occasionally, Ivan favored them with a solo in his still fine basso voice, but he preferred for his guests to sing. And they did, especially late at night when the vodka and wines from the Crimea flowed and the most boisterous dancing began.

Well known at the restaurant, patrons greeted Paul and his family with loud calls and classic bear hugs. Ivan's voice boomed over the noise as he quickly led them to tables reserved for them. "So you are Henri Stephenovich," he said, holding Henri's shoulders in his huge hands. "We have heard about you. Welcome to our restaurant. Melushka, come see whom Paul Edourdovich has brought," he called to his wife. She immediately appeared at the kitchen door, red-cheeked from the heat from her enormous Aga. "He has brought his young nephew, Henri Stephenovich. Anna, Sophie, Marie, Vanya, Vashya, come and meet the new nephew just back from the war." Ivan's family surrounded Henri as Ivan led him off to the table.

Paul stood and in a booming voice asked, "Are all you men hungry?" When heads nodded eagerly, he laughed. "Good. I've ordered a true Russian meal for you, a meal fit for the Tsars. We'll begin with *Okroshka,* a cold cucumber soup with game and herbs in kvas and cream. The next course will be a crayfish soufflé and after that comes *Tushenaia Kuritsa Pod Sousam iz Chernosliv,* which translated means a braised chicken with a sauce made of prunes. I think you will enjoy this as it is truly delicious." Paul paused frowning slightly. "Let me think; what did I order next? Ah! Yes. I ordered two kinds of meat for you: braised veal with caviar sauce and skewered pork with pomegranate syrup. These are called *Teliatynaz Pidlyvolu iz Ikry* and *Karabakh Khorovats',* respectively. We usually serve the vegetables as a separate course and for this I ordered *Sabzi Piez,* which are braised onions and carrots, and also Karabakjh Loby, string beans in sour cream and tomato sauce. Dessert is a Charlottka, a ladyfinger mold with a cream filling, also known as a Charlotte Russe. As I said, I hope you are all hungry!"

Paul and Ivan conferred on the wines to be served, deciding upon a sherry after the soup; a Caucasian red wine from Ivan's special stock in his wine cellar to accompany the meat courses; and a lovely Tokay with the dessert.

After Paul ordered the wines, he led his guests to the Zakuska table. "The custom of always having a table of this type in one's country home originated several centuries ago when guests arrived unexpectedly. More than likely, they had traveled over long distances, often in subzero weather, and they would be cold, tired and above all hungry. The table was always kept ready for just such an event. One's guests were served this light meal while waiting for dinner to be prepared. The table grew over a period of time until it became fashionable in St. Petersburg at the turn of this century to have a substantial meal, go to the theatre, then eat a late dinner, much like an English or Scottish high tea before the theatre with super to follow.

"But the best part of the Zakuska is the vodka! Usually there are fifteen to twenty different kinds," Paul went on to explain to his fascinated audience. "*Krasnaia Golovka* is the best clear vodka and is made by steeping two or three stalks of Buffalo grass in a bottle of vodka, turning it the color of new hay; another of the favorites is *Rubinovaia* which is a brilliant orange color, made with berries of the mountain ash; then there is a mauve colored vodka made from litmus lichen; a lemon vodka made from a long peel pared from a single lemon; and *Samrodinovka*, which is a ruby color and *Pestsovka* which is fortified with black pepper. These my young friends are just a few of the vodkas."

Paul smiled as he watched the varied expressions on the young faces around him, ranging from incredulous to delight. "But, of course, those who partake of a very hearty Zakuska and drink a lot of vodka may afterwards finish with a glass of English ale, which restores the appetite and helps to sober them up." He laughed heartily when he saw total amazement on the faces of his audience. "Now, let me demonstrate how to eat a Zakuska. First, you pour a small glass of chilled vodka. Never sip vodka, always drink it in one gulp. Then you have a bite of caviar or this *pashtet*. Then you have another glass of vodka and a taste of herring, another glass of vodka and so it goes. Now enjoy yourselves, but remember, you will be eating a six course meal afterwards," he admonished.

At this, the men started on the Zakuska with a will until dinner was ready. The Troop sat at two long tables with Henri at the head of one. Paul was with General Dayton, the Colonel, the Doctor and the Captain along with Alicia and Maria at a separate table, while Carlotta elected to sit with the men and headed the other long table. Alexei and Jean also sat with the Troop.

Young Maria shone with excitement. Only fourteen-years-old, this was her first grown up event. Henri, had told her that she looked beautiful, a picture of their mother as he remembered her. Never having known her mother, she cherished the small oval framed picture that sat on her dresser at home. Henri's remark had made the event all the more special for her.

Between courses and after the meal, each member of the family was asked to sing, and later the dancing started. With much hilarity, Carlotta, Maria, Jean and Alexei tried to teach the members of the Troop how to do the Russian dances. Vanya, Vashya, Anna, Sophie and Marie tried also, but all ended up in uncontrollable laughter. Henri had danced with the rest, but now he sat at his uncle's side watching with a smile on his lips but none in his eyes.

Paul had been observing Henri all evening and noticed he joined into the general hilarity, but his heart did not seem to be in it. A cloud occasionally passed across his face and his eyes took on a far away look. Paul put his hand on Henri's outstretched arm as Henri played with an empty glass. "What are you thinking about?"

"Nothing really, just watching the rest," Henri replied, giving his uncle a fleeting smile.

"Who is Ladislaus and who are Jan and Yurick?" Paul persisted.

Henri gave him a quick look, "You are quite perceptive, or else you are starting to know me too well," he said, then, reached out, poured himself another glass of vodka and leaned back in his chair. "Ladislaus was an Hungarian resistance fighter during the war. He had been a Colonel in the cavalry and is from the old landed aristocracy. Jan and Yurick were also army men, artillery, and also resistance fighters."

"And when did you meet them?

"Just after I started working for M15 my superiors sent me to Hungary to make contact with the resistance leaders and to learn the situation there. Amongst other things, I was to set up a clandestine radio network. That's when I met Ladislaus. We worked closely together for a couple of months...then I left again."

"Did you go back?"

"Yes, several times. The man is fantastic, Uncle Paul. If I could be half the man he is, I would be happy. He has the courage, strength and fighting spirit that few men possess, and the brains to use them correctly. All the men under him loved him and would do anything for him. He is a born leader and one I would follow gladly."

Paul, watching his nephew's face, remembered a great number of men saying the same thing about Henri. He smiled to himself. Paul also knew that Ladislaus must be quite a person for his nephew to say this of him, for Henri would never willingly follow anyone unless he had full trust in him.

"The last time I was in Hungary was just before the Red Army came through," Henri went on half musingly. "I knew they were looking for Ladislaus, and were a greater threat to him than the Germans. I tried to find him, to try to persuade him to leave with me, but he had disappeared and I wasn't able to warn him. I left messages in various places, but finally I could wait no longer, I had to leave. Tonight, he told me that he had deliberately instructed his people not to let me know where he was because it would have been too dangerous for me!" Henri laughed slightly. "While in Vienna, I talked with various people who had fled Hungary after the Russian occupation. They knew Ladislaus, and all of them said he had been killed. That's why I was so astonished to see him tonight."

"Who is Mary?"

"His wife. She's Swiss and they had been married only a few months when I first knew them. When she became pregnant, Ladislaus insisted she go back to Switzerland for the birth and to stay there during the war. When I left the first time, I took her with me, and after the baby was born, stood Godfather to their son."

"What is he doing now? Paul asked.

Henri shrugged his shoulders, "I really don't know," he answered evasively.

"He's leading or directing a resistance movement against the Communists, is he not, Henri?"

Henri flashed a smile and said quietly, his eyes suddenly becoming veiled, "Perhaps." Before Paul could question him further, Henri rose moving onto the dance floor to dance the *Kazachka* and avoided any more *tete-a-tetes* with Paul for the rest of the evening.

120

The show went on with no incidents and Henri's two shadows began to think that all would be well. After all, who would take the risk of attacking Henri when he was constantly surrounded by Academy men or members of his family? Henri himself kept his guard up. He had the feeling of being watched and was careful to leave no openings for an attacker. The only way he could be shot was from the stands and they were well covered. He knew men watched the alleyway and the shadows kept their eyes on the stable area.

During the day, Henri showed the men around London. They found a carnival on the outskirts one night after the show, and almost wiped out the shooting galleries. Sometimes they invited the girls they met to join them on these excursions along with Carlotta and Maria.

Afternoons and evenings were taken up with the show, and here the Academy men were doing well. The team posted the highest score so far for their events. Pantelon and Blackbird were tied for the highest score of the individual Jumpers.

Henri kept his promise to do only the less dangerous tricks in his nightly Cossack riding. He no longer wore the full Cossack costume, only the blouse and sash, as this gave him more freedom of movement.

On the last night, Jimmy had Pantelon saddled and ready for him. Jimmy always went out to watch the Special Riding event. Tonight was no exception. All the Academy men gathered either in the alleyway or scattered throughout the stands to watch the Jumpers. The shadows had also stepped outside into the alleyway, leaving the stable area deserted.

Believing the area to be under someone's eye, Henri whistled happily to himself as he stepped into the stall he used for changing and stripped off his blouse. A slight sound behind him brought him to attention and as he began to turn he felt a searing pain as a knife plunged into his left shoulder. Staggering, he fell and by the time he righted himself, the sound of his assailant's footsteps faded in the distance. Pursuit was useless.

Cursing himself for a fool for relaxing his guard, he managed to sit up on the bed and twist his head around in order to see the damage to his back in the mirror. Hearing Jimmy approach, he called out, "Jimmy, come in here a minute will you?"

"Cor! What happened?"

"Don't ask questions. Get me a clean wet cloth and bring the first aid kit."

"Oughtn't I to call a doctor?"

"No! Just do as I say and stop talking."

Jimmy cleaned the wound and bandaged it. Henri was beginning to feel a little sick, but fought it.

"Mr. Bolkonsky, you aren't thinking of riding Pantelon are you?"

"We can't change riders now. It's against the rules and we'd loose all the points we've won so far," Henri said. "Now hold Pantelon still and give me a leg up." Henri swung into the saddle gathering the reins in his right hand, his face pale but grim. "I want you to promise you won't say anything about this to anyone until the event is over."

"What if you get hurt out in the ring? Captain Harding will have my neck if I've kept it from him."

"I'll take full responsibility for my decision, Jimmy. You will not be blamed. I'll see to that. Now promise."

"Okay, Mr. Bolkonsky, but I think you're crazy to try this."

Henri sat behind the gate waiting. Blackbird was the only horse with a clean jump on his first go round. All the others had two or more faults so far. Henri felt he could at least tie that the first time, but he worried about jump offs. The course held twelve jumps, most with six-foot spreads, except the fourteen foot water jump. He had enough strength now, but he knew he would weaken as he rode.

Henri picked up the reins and, shortening them, pulled Pantelon's head up. All set, he nodded his head for the men to open the gates. He didn't bother to make the customary circle, but headed Pantelon directly into the first jump. Pantelon, as usual, fought him all the way and it became increasingly difficult to control him with only one hand. He finished the course and smiled when he heard the announcer say, "Clean round for No. 7. That makes two horses with clean rounds for the jump off: No. 2

Blackbird ridden by Jean Bolkonsky and No. 7 Pantelon ridden by Henri Bolkonsky. There will be a jump off against time."

When Henri rode into the ring, Paul knew at once that something was wrong. Even Sergei noticed, and leaned over from his box commenting that Henri had failed to ride the opening circle. Paul assured him that the problem was a result of riding hard all week, late nights and not enough sleep.

Now, they waited for the first jump off. Nine jumps were raised to five feet seven and five feet nine inches. Directly in front of the family's box was the most difficult jump, a combination with the first fence, an upright, five feet three inches; the second, an oxer, five feet seven; and the third, another oxer, five feet nine. The difficulty lay in that the horses had only one non-jumping stride before the first oxer and two non-jumping strides before the second.

Paul smiled proudly as Blackbird took the jumps cleanly. "Time…thirty one point six seconds," intoned the announcer.

When Henri moved Pantelon into the ring this time, Paul knew something was definitely wrong and it had nothing to do with late nights. He signaled Igor and Pyotr, already moving toward the alleyway and the exit gate; they didn't need to be told.

It had taken some time for Henri to shorten the reins on Pantelon, who kept stretching his neck forward before Henri could get a good grip on them. He finally got them tight enough, this time wrapping them around his right hand to ensure their staying tight. When the gates opened, he had a hard time making Pantelon walk into the first jump. On the second, the water jump, it felt as if Pantelon was going to pull his arm out of its socket, but they made it over cleanly.

The jarring on his left shoulder caused his head to swim. Henri willed himself and Pantelon over the jumps, fighting the pain and nausea which threatened to overcome him. They landed wrong on the seventh jump and the eighth was coming up too fast. Henri hauled back hard on the reins pulling Pantelon almost to a standstill. He knew his timing was off as Pantelon lifted under him. He heard Pantelon tick the jump hard as they went over but he didn't dare look back.

"Only one more," he kept repeating to himself as he headed into the combination. He had little time and room to pull Pantelon in and the horse started to sidestep. Henri had to make him go in straight, otherwise, he would refuse it. Now, he gave up all pretense. He combined kicking Pantelon in the side and reined in his neck and managed to straighten him out. When he released Pantelon, the horse took the upright beautifully, then knocked the bar off the first oxer but managed to clear the second. "Four faults for No. 7. Time…thirty two-seconds."

Henri yelled to the gate people, "heads up," unwinding the reins from his hand. He wanted to get out of the ring before he passed out completely. He managed to pull the horse in just as Pyotr leaped, grabbing the reins to stop him. Igor caught Henri as he slid out of the saddle. Jean put his arm around his cousin's waist helping to hold him upright.

"What happened, your highness?" Igor asked.

Leaning heavily against him, "Where is Chris?" Henri asked.

"Right here. What happened?"

"Take Pantelon in to pick up the ribbon, will you, Chris? I can't make it," he said, adding with a twisted smile, "Sorry about the trophy."

"Never mind that. What in hell happened?"

"Never mind now, just get into the ring, will you"

Jean tightened his hold, "Can you get to the first aid station?"

"The room in the stable area is closer. I think I can make that. You better go back to the ring too."

"The hell with that!"

"Go! Igor can help me." Henri gave Jean a weak grin and a reassuring nod. "By the way, congratulations. Now, get going, will you?" Alicia and Alexei came up with Paul, and they almost pushed Jean back through the gate.

Alicia hurried on ahead to see that the room was ready as Alexei raced for the doctor. Igor and Pyotr, on either side of Henri, half carried, half walked him to the room where he collapsed full length on the bed.

Henri repeated to the doctor exactly what had happened. "It's a damn good thing you turned around as you did; otherwise, that knife would have done a great deal more damage. It could have been fatal."

Not until Alicia was satisfied that Henri was resting comfortably, did she allow Captain Harding to come in. "Why did you ride?" he asked. "You should have called the doctor immediately."

"We were too close to winning the trophy," Henri said. "I just didn't count on the jump off being so difficult."

"You're an idiot!" Harding replied, but with a smile on his lips.

"I know, but it was for the greater glory of the Academy," Henri laughed.

Paul came to collect Henri and drive him to the hotel. He made arrangements to get a single room for him where Alicia and Igor could look after him for the night, and Captain Harding made arrangements to have a bed made up for him on the train back to the Academy early the next morning, all of which Henri protested, to no avail. He finally had to give in to their combined numbers.

"The police looked," Paul said, "but they couldn't find anything in the area that might have pointed to anyone as your attacker."

"I'm not surprised."

"You must be careful, nephew. He and others are still out there."

Chapter 13

The day Henri left the hospital at the Academy, he sensed someone nearby...watching him. He had been shadowed for too many years not to trust his instincts now. This time, he knew, his enemies...waiting and biding their time...would make no mistakes. He stayed away from all open areas where there was a clear shot from the woods or hills and was alert and suspicious of all strangers and cars that came to the Academy. He knew he had become lax in London, enjoying himself as he had been, showing London to the men and riding in the show. He cursed himself for that, but now he returned to vigilance.

His close friends kept him surrounded at all times during this period, even Velp, Leonardo and Ferranto unobtrusively kept their eyes on him and, with the others, helped guard him.

June was still two months away, but with every passing day, Henri became a little more tense and nervous. He hated the thought of the trials coming up. He felt the need to be alone with his own somber thoughts, but it was impossible for him to get away. Only when he rode Vlaska could he relax. Even then, he couldn't canter over the rolling moors or along the edge of the Loch by himself. His feeling of being caged grew with each day and he became more edgy and irritable.

During the day, he buried himself in his work and studies, concentrating on perfecting his abilities with the foil, rapier and saber, or practicing judo and Karate with his friends, and working out in gymnastics, hoping that with physical exhaustion he would be able to clear his mind and sleep. But inevitably with "lights out," he found himself alone with his thoughts...memories which he had kept at bay during his waking hours, came flooding back into his consciousness with a vengeance and night after night, he lay awake for hours before drifting into a troubled sleep.

Soon after his return, Henri heard the Gypsies were back. He and several other men left the Academy late one Friday afternoon after classes, planning to camp overnight with them. The men gave their horses their heads across the moors letting them work off the first spurts of energy. Vlaska quickly drew ahead of the rest. The feel of the wind against his face, the powerful horse under him, the open spaces and the warm sun on his back made Henri feel alive again.

He reluctantly reined Vlaska in, slowing his pace as Mario drew up alongside and the two continued on together at a slow canter. A few pale green leaves were beginning to show themselves on the bushes and the first scent of heather hung in the air. Spring had come late, but seemed to be rapidly catching up. The horses moved over the damp ground as their riders enjoyed the warmth and the fresh air. The two men finally slowed their mounts to a walk, waiting for the others to catch up with them.

"I've been curious about some of the things I saw and heard in London," Mario said, breaking the silence between them.

Henri glanced at him with a half smile. "Such as?"

"Well, for instance, you have mentioned the term Cossack several times, and you say you have been trained by them Who exactly are they and where do they come from?"

Henri grinned, "That's a little hard to explain unless you know something of Russian history. Briefly, the Tartars, or Mongols, held sway in the Crimea on the Black Sea, Kazan and Astrakhan on the Volga, until about fifteen seventy-one. The Tartars were nomads who roamed with their herds throughout the steppe area. The Russians pushed down toward this fertile land, and a shifting frontier developed between them. The Cossacks, mostly freebooters who found plundering and fighting more profitable than farming, came into being here. Some of the Cossacks, I would say most of them, were serfs who had run away from their masters, others were murderers and thieves wanted by the law. The two largest groups established themselves in this no-man's land between the settled area and the nomads. One group on the Dnieper River, became known as Zaporogian Cossacks. The other main group, the Don Cossacks, got their name from the river they lived beside, the Don.

127

Igor, Pyotr and their family are Don Cossacks. These two groups often plundered ships that traded up and down the rivers. The Tsars sent armies to wipe out, or at least subdue them, but without much success. The Cossacks have a turbulent history. They fought for whoever paid the highest, or for some wild and crazy cause, if it struck their fancy. They led many peasant revolts against the domination of the Tsars, but in the end the Tsars tamed them somewhat. Eventually, they became an integral part of the Imperial Army and probably the most feared of all the troops. They had the same sort of reputation as the Gurkahs have with the British army today."

Mario continued to ply Henri with questions, and the two men became involved in deep conversation on Russian history and traditions. They moved along a small, almost invisible, path, their slow canter allowing them to talk. Suddenly, both horses threw their heads snorting in surprise. Six men blocked their path. Swiftly, Henri and Mario turned their mounts around but five more horsemen stood in a rough semi-circle behind them, cutting them off from their friends, who were too far back to witness the attack.

Henri turned Vlaska's head across the hill, calling for Mario to follow. He hoped to be able to swing around the men, break out into the open and join up with the others. The two men plunged across the hill, lying low along their horses' necks, while several rifles opened up. Bullets spattered into the ground around them, but none hit the riders. Fleetingly, Henri wondered where their companions were as he and Mario dashed for freedom. Once again, he cursed himself for carelessly having ridden so far ahead.

Mario looked up the hill, "Watch out, Henri, several riders are moving at an angle, trying to cut us off!"

They whipped their horses faster now, heedless of the terrain they dashed over. In the lead, Henri heard a yell and, looking back, saw Mario surrounded. He pulled Vlaska to a rearing halt and turning back, rode into the rear of the group, slashing at the men with his riding crop, trying to clear a path for Mario. His sudden assault momentarily startled their assailants, enough so that Mario was able to come up to his side.

The two horses reared and plunged, frightened by the smell of blood and the smashing of horse against horse. At a touch of Henri's heels, Vlaska reared as commanded, lashed out with his forelegs knocking one of the men who blocked their path to the ground. They broke free, only to be surrounded again by the other four riders. Henri and Mario fought hard, but the odds against them were too great. The last thing Henri remembered was seeing Mario viciously knocked from his horse before he felt excruciating pain at the back of his head and oblivion.

When Henri awoke, he found himself bound to a rough wooden bed in a small room. Grey light filtered through a dust-laden window onto a dirt floor. Tentatively, he moved his head only to be rewarded with a blinding flash of pain. When he could see again, he carefully moved his eyes over the room, bare except for another wooden bed like the one on which he lay. Mario, bound to it hand and foot, appeared to be asleep.

The only door to the room suddenly opened crashing back against the wooden wall. A massive figure stood framed in the doorway, his head almost touching the lintel. Henri's eyes narrowed to mere slits as he watched the man advance toward his bed. He could smell sour breath as rough fingers checked his pulse. The man seemed satisfied and walked over to the other bed to check Mario. With a final glance back in Henri's direction, he left the room.

Henri allowed a few minutes to pass before whispering, "Mario, are you awake?" When he received no reply, he tested the bonds that held him but found he couldn't work the knots loose. He felt for the knife he always had strapped to his wrist hoping his captors had not found it, but knowing this hope was fruitless.

The room slipped into darkness as he lay contemplating what he could do to get them out of their predicament. He wondered what had happened to the men who had been following them and where they were now. Almost immediately, he stopped this useless train of thought and, for what seemed to him a long time, considered various plans, rejecting most of them. When he heard a movement from the other bed, he whispered, "Mario, are you all right?" A soft groan came as reply. He asked again, more urgently, "Mario, are you okay?"

"I think so. What about you?"

"Other than a rather large headache, I'm fine."

"Where the hell are we?"

"I'm not sure, but I think a deserted cabin somewhere in the hills behind the Academy." He stopped. "Hush! Someone is coming. Pretend to be asleep."

His warning came too late, for again the door crashed open. Three men strode into the room, one of them carrying a kerosene lamp. "So our two sleeping beauties have finally awakened," one of them said in a deep guttural voice. "We have a few questions to ask you."

The other two bent down, loosened Henri's bonds and jerked him to his feet. His head began to swim from the sudden movement, but at least the pain had subsided to a dull ache. He allowed himself to be led part way across the room, when he suddenly jerked free chopping one man in the neck, killing him. He swiftly turned on the other chopping him across the throat, killing him also. Three more men rushed into the room in answer to a yell from the one holding the lantern. The three of them wrestled Henri to the floor while the guttural voiced one bound his hands behind his back.

They dragged him, struggling, into the next room and bound him to a chair. The big man whom Henri had seen earlier, sat in a chair behind a table watching him with cold amusement. "I can see your reputation is richly deserved, but you might as well give up this time. You must see you are badly outnumbered and resistance is worse than useless," he drawled.

Henri said nothing, but watched with cold hooded eyes. He had seen Dietrich only twice before in his life and knew his bloody reputation only too well: Heydrich's right hand man, then Himmler's after Heydrich's death; chief organizer of the massacre at Babi Yar; coordinator of the round up, torture and death of those even remotely involved in the July 20th plot; escaped from Nuremberg prison; reputed to be in the higher echelons of the Deutches Gemenshaft. Dietrich had close cropped pale blond hair. Under the kerosene lamp, hanging from the ceiling, he looked almost bald. His grey eyes, under pale blond eyebrows, were as wintery as the North Sea. His mouth habitually turned down at the corners, as deep lines ran from his nose to his lips and across his pale, badly pockmarked face.

Henri, fully realizing the desperate situation both he and Mario were in, stalled for time "Where are the rest of your cohorts?"

"I sent most of them back. I don't think we'll need them from now on." Dietrich smiled. "Now my young friend, we wish to know a few things, but first, I warn you, I will only ask the questions once. If you do not answer, my subordinates will see that you do and, as you know, they are not gentle. Do you understand me?"

Henri's lips tightened, his eyes equally as cold as the ones he met. "Yes, I understand you well, Dietrich, but you are wasting your time."

"I see." Dietrich leaned back with a slight sigh. "I have heard you are a very stubborn man." With a sign, one of the men who stood behind Henri came forward. "Do you know what this is?" Dietrich asked, holding up a rope which had been tied into several knots. "It is rather medieval, but we have found it helps to persuade people to talk."

He tossed the rope to the man who placed it around Henri's forehead. Slipping a long wooden peg between the rope and Henri's head, he began to twist the circlet. The knots pressed into Henri's temples and forehead until Henri thought his brain was going to be squeezed from his skull. He closed his eyes against the pain, biting back the screams rising in his throat; fighting back with the only thing he had…his silence.

The release from pain was almost as bad as the pain itself. Henri slumped forward against the ropes binding him to the chair. When the roaring subsided in his ears, he heard Dietrich saying, "Now, Mr. Bolkonsky, will you answer my questions?" with venomous hatred in his eyes, Henri shook his head.

At another sign from d\Dietrich, the rope tightened around Henri's temples again. He could feel blood running down his forehead into his eyes and mouth. He remembered vaguely thinking it tasted salty. Finally, Henri sank unconscious against his bonds.

Cautiously, Henri moved his body, finding he was lying on the earth floor, his face caked with a mixture of blood and dirt. A soft groan escaped him as he became conscious of sharp throbbing pains in his head.

"Henri, what happened? Are you all right?" Mario's anxious whisper came through the darkness.

With an effort, trying to make his voice sound normal, he replied, "Yes, so far. Keep talking so I can locate you. My hands and feet are tied, but otherwise, I'm free."

"What happened out there? I couldn't hear anything for a long time, then the door opened and they threw you back in here."

Henri rolled over to Mario's bedside and started to hoist himself up. "Keep your ear cocked for any noise. I'm going to try to loosen your wrists. When I do, I want you to free yourself. They will probably be back in a little while to question me further. Once you're free, loosen my bonds. There's an off chance we can both get out of here together before they come back, but I doubt it. If not, while I'm gone, I want you to get out that window without making a noise, and go for help. Do you understand?"

"Yes, but what about you? I can't leave here without you."

"You can and you will! You'll have to use something to make it look as if you're still here. I'll try to hold on and not pass out as long as I can to give you time, but for God's sake, hurry."

While they talked, Henri untied the ropes around Mario's wrists. "I have an amulet on a chain around my neck. Take it with you. The Gypsy encampment should not be far away. It's probably closer than the Academy. You can spot it by their fires. Give the amulet to the leader, Liubov, and tell him what has happened. He will send help. It looks like only five men are left here." Henri paused to listen then went on hurriedly. "Remember the name Dietrich. He is the one running the show here as he did in Czechoslovakia during the war. He is on the wanted list of Nazis and he was just below Heydrich."

Henri slipped back onto the floor, rolling back just in time to where he had been when he regained consciousness. Again the door slammed open. Men pulled him roughly to his feet and dragged him into the next room.

After several false starts, Mario untied his feet. When he was free, he silently crossed to the door and peered through a crack between the boards. Henri was tied to the table in the middle of the room, face down. One of the men raised his arm, bringing a thick leather belt down in a vicious blow across his back. Mario saw Henri's head jerk up in pain as he bit his lips to keep from crying out. Deep red welts striped his back and blood flowed down his sides. Mario cursed under his breath. *I can't leave him here to be whipped to death and I can't take on all the men in that room single handedly without a weapon.* He a pack of matches from his trouser pocket and a smile slipped across his face. Swiftly, he jimmied the window open, hoisted himself up and dropped to the ground. After a quick search, he found enough dry brush to start a good fire. Shielding the tiny flame from the wind, he set alight the brush he had piled against the windowless portion of the wall. As soon as it was going well, he raced back to the window and re-entered the room.

Again he peered through the crack. One of the men threw water into Henri's face to bring him around. Mario prayed silently that the wall would catch quickly before they could do any more damage. He crossed his fingers when he heard one of the men say, "I smell smoke." All but one man raced from the room. Mario silently opened the door and, with a flying leap, landed on the remaining man. With a sharp right, he knocked him out before he could give a warning.

Mario's searching fingers found a knife on the unconscious man. Swiftly, cutting the bonds tying Henri to the table, he slipped an arm under him. As Mario carried Henri into their prison room, he noticed the dry brittle wood of the old cabin burned well. *It will take them some time before they can put it out, if at all, h*e thought with satisfaction. Henri began to come around as Mario wedged the two beds against the door.

"Henri, can you stand on your feet?"

"Ja. I think so," he answered through clenched teeth.

"Come on then, we're got to get out of here before this hut goes up in flames completely."

With Mario's help, Henri staggered to the window, hoisted himself up and then dropped to the ground. As Mario slipped through after him, Henri heard the men trying to break down the door into the room. Dark clouds covered the sky hiding the moon. The cold fresh air began to clear Henri's head as he and Mario crouched against the wall. Mario slipped an arm around Henri's waist, and bending low, they raced across the ground. The hilly ground offered little cover but, if they moved carefully, it provided enough shallow ravines to hide them from their pursuers,. They dropped into one of the small ravines, turned left keeping to its bottom and running as best they could to put as much distance between them and the blazing hut as possible.

Finally, Henri, gasping for breath, called a halt. He collapsed to the ground, partially hidden by some scrub brush, unable to move. Mario's breath came with difficulty also, as he hunkered down beside Henri. When Henri began to shiver uncontrollably, as much from the chill wind biting into his body as from the adrenaline pumped into him and the delayed shock from the whipping, Mario slipped his jacket off and laid it over Henri's back. "This will give you a little warmth. Where do we go from here?" Looking around in the dim light, he continued, "I have no idea even in which direction to head."

Nodding his thanks for the jacket, Henri said, "We'll have to crawl up to the top of that hill over there. Perhaps, we can get our bearings. In a way this cloud cover is a blessing but…" He didn't finish the sentence for his sharp ears had picked up the sound of footsteps coming in their direction. Mario immediately flattened himself along the ground beside Henri in answer to Henri's silent gesture. Noiselessly, they crawled toward better cover a short distance away.

Against the faint glow of the still blazing hut, they saw the dim outline of two men standing at the top of the ravine. Presently, two more joined them, all looking toward the fire. When a fifth man joined the group, Henri recognized Liubov. Almost crying out with joy, he slipped from his hiding place and started toward them. Halfway across the distance that separated them, he suddenly threw himself flat to the ground pulling Mario down with him. Two more men had appeared and one of them was Dietrich. Henri held his breath praying they had not been seen.

Too far to tell what Dietrich was saying, Henri watched as he gestured with his hands, nearly shouting, while Liubov appeared to be playing dumb. Dietrich shook his head, eloquently shrugged his shoulders spreading his hands wide. Liubov turned away, signaling his men to follow and heading straight for the place where Henri and Mario lay under a small heather bush. Dietrich stood where they left him, watching the little group as they noisily strode toward the bottom of the ravine. As Liubov passed by, he whispered to Henri, "Stay where you are. We will come back for you."

Half an hour later, Henri heard the unmistakable sounds of horses. Looking up as they came nearer, he saw Liubov and seven of his men coming along the bottom of the ravine. "Well, Boyar, you have had a fine time of it tonight. Mount quickly for your enemies are still about," Liubov greeted him softly. Henri and Mario needed no encouragement, and the group turned their heads for the gypsy encampment back along the ravine.

Chapter 14

The *vardos* were parked in an open-ended square, with Liubov's, by far the largest, at the head. A small fire burned in front of each, fueled by the large communal blaze in the center of the square. Dogs yapped noisily as the men rode in, but were quickly quieted with a well-aimed stick.

Henri smiled when he saw Lita standing quietly waiting to welcome him. That wonderful night he had spent with her and the rest of the Gypsies seemed so long ago. Now, she and Liubov's wife, Sonia, washed, cleaned and bandaged Henri's head and back, made him drink some potion Sonia made up and put him to bed. Mario, sitting in the vardo, marveled at Henri's endurance. He didn't cry out or make a sound as the women took care of his back. Mario knew it must be extremely painful, for some of the gashes were deep. The only signs Henri gave were a tightening of his lips, or a quick intake of breath through his clenched teeth. Lita shooed them all out when she and Sonia had finished, firmly closing the door.

Liubov led Mario to his vardo, where they sat talking on its steps for a long time. Mario told Liubov what had happened, concluding with, "He turned back to save me when he was out in the clear and could have gotten away. I owe him my life twice over and then some. He is due to leave for the trials in a month and a half, and until he is delivered into the army's hands, somehow he has got to be so well protected and hidden that not even a mouse could get to him.

Liubov, pulling on his pipe silently nodded. His face had seemed made of stone as he listened to Mario's tale. Now, he turned brilliant dark eyes on him, "He can stay here with us. They would never think to look for this Boyar amongst Romabichals.

He is tanned enough, though we can darken his skin more. Only his eyes will give him away. For the first week or so, he will have to stay in bed anyway, and by then we will be well away to the North."

For the first time that day, Mario relaxed a little and felt Henri might be safe. "Thank you. It's just possible that would be the best plan." He paused for a second and then went on almost to himself. "He is one of the very rare people who walk this earth. If you are very lucky, and meet one of them, you will give up all to follow where they lead, and lay down your life in their service." He stopped embarrassed by what he had just said and fixedly stared at the fire.

Liubov only smiled in understanding. "Do not be afraid of emotions. We Gypsies are known for our temperaments. We let everyone know how we feel, from fiery to lyrical. We never hold anything back and we are more contented than you, for we never become frustrated." His white teeth gleamed through his black beard as he watched Mario with sparkling eyes. "Your friend, lying in Lita's vargo, is much the same, for he is a true Russian by nature." Liubov rose, stretched, knocked the ashes from his pipe and yawned. "It is time for you to sleep. My wife has prepared a place for you in our vardo for tonight. Tomorrow, you shall go back to the Academy and ease the minds of his friends there."

When Henri woke from a deep two-day sleep, he found Lita sitting at his bedside. He lay on the hard double bed at one end of the caravan, an old fashioned down quilt tucked around him. Heavy curtains were drawn across small windows shutting out the dark night. A table, pulled down at the far end, effectively blocked the only door. A shaded overhead paraffin lamp cast a bright circle on two men sitting playing cards. Another lamp on the bedside table cast a light over an earthenware pitcher and a glass. The rest of the *vardo* was in deep shadow, the only sound coming from the cards flicked on the table.

As soon as Henri opened his eyes, Lita put down her sewing and moved over to sit on the edge of the bed. She checked his pulse and temperature with an expert air. Slowly, Henri's mind caught up with his eyes and he became fully conscious of everything around him.

"How do you feel?"

"All right. Where am I?" Henri tried to sit up, but the bandages around his chest and back restricted his movements.

Lita helped him, fixing some pillows behind him, "You are in my *vardo*." She put her hand out quickly as Henri started to lean back. "Go slowly, Boyar. Do not lean back too quickly," she warned.

"What was in that potion Sonia gave me?" Henri was becoming somewhat alarmed, especially when he caught sight of wicked looking *churls* stuck into the belts of the two card players.

"She gave you a special mixture to help you sleep and heal more quickly." Lita sat back on the bed clasping one knee in her hands, a secret amused little smile touching her lips.

"Why am I still here at the camp and not the Academy?" Henri asked slowly, putting his hand up to his aching head and feeling the bandages wrapped around his forehead.

"I do not know. You are full of questions, Boyar." Looking over her shoulder, she called, "Lonya, tell Liubov the Boyar is awake."

One of the card players looked up and grunted. He slowly rose from his chair, peered in Henri's direction, then left. Lita left the *vardo*, only to return minutes later with a steaming bowl of soup. "Drink this, Boyar, it will give you strength." She slowly spooned the thick, rich liquid into Henri's mouth.

Henri looked up quickly as Liubov entered the *vardo* filling it with his presence. "Good evening, how are you feeling?"

"As well as can be expected," Henri gave him a wry smile. "I think a little better." He hesitated for a moment, his eyes flickering over the other men in the room.

"All of you, out!" Liubov ordered. As soon as they were alone, he sat on the edge of the bed, regarding Henri with interest. "Your friends at the Academy know where you are so you need not worry about them."

"I'm confused as to why I'm still here instead of at the Academy," Henri said slowly, looking directly at Liubov's eyes.

138

"We have decided you will be safer here where no one can get to you without our knowing it."

"But that is putting you and your people in danger."

"Who would think to look for you, Boyar, amongst *Romanichals*?" His eyes sparkled in amusement.

"Dietrich is no fool, Liubov. He knows there were only two places I could have gone that night: to the Academy or to your camp. He will soon discover I am not at the Academy, and then he will come looking for you."

"There are many camps like this one where you can hide safely."

"And what makes you think the others will take me in?"

"The amulet you wear. That is your passport. *Romanichals* anywhere in the world will look after you as long as you have it."

"Thank you, Liubov, but all of you are endangered now."

"I owe you this, Boyar."

"You owe me nothing."

"I owe you much more. Without your help, we would all be dead." Liubov held up his hand. "No, do not argue with me, Boyar. You will stay with us. My sons," he nodded toward the door, "will stay with you and guard you with their lives."

Laying back on the pillow, Henri was tiring fast. His semi-drugged brain moved sluggishly. He closed his eyes for a minute, trying to think clearly. When he opened them, Loubov had risen. "You are tired and I have stayed too long. Rest now. When you awaken again, you will be better. Your friend, Mario, will come back this weekend before we move on. Is there anything you especially want?"

Henri started to say something then shook his head. "Has my family been informed as to where I am?"

"Yes, your friend called them. They seem to agree with us about your safety." He paused, searching Henri's face with keen sharp eyes. "You did think of something. What was it?"

"*Nichevo*...nothing important. Thank you, Liubov."

"All right. Rest now." Liubov left the room sending Lita back in with his two sons. Henri was only partially aware of her hovering over him and suspected the soup she had given him had been drugged. Within minutes, he dropped into a deep sleep.

Mario arrived at the Gypsies' new campsite early Friday night right after classes were over. He found Henri sitting up in bed watching Lita move about the *vardo*. Liubov's two sons sat on the steps smoking and rose as Mario approached, their hands hovering over the handles of their churis. Lita moved swiftly to the door and said something in a low voice, which Henri didn't quite catch, for she spoke in her own language. Although Henri spoke fluent Russian, this was Romany, a language unto itself. He was only partially familiar with it, but in the weeks to come would become more fluent.

Mario ran up the stairs, and he approached the bed. "Hello, how are you feeling?"

"Fine. What about you?" Henri smiled, happy to see him again.

"Liubov's wife says you are doing well, and you do look a lot better."

"Thanks. Sit down." Henri indicated a place on the edge of the bed. "I've been anxious to see you again. You had better be prepared for I have a thousand and one questions for you."

"Before you start, let me say that everyone has been worried about you and they all send their best." Mario grinned. "Even Burt and Steve."

"What happened to the rest? Where were they when the fight took place?"

"We had gotten quite a way ahead of them without realizing it and had disappeared over the rise of a hill. Remember the fork in the dirt track we were following?" Henri nodded. "Well, we took the left track and they the right. By the time they realized their mistake, the fight must have been over."

"What happened then?"

"They backtracked, took the left fork and arrived at camp all right, but when they found we weren't there, they really got upset. They and the Gypsies went out to comb the hills, but couldn't find us. They tore back to the Academy and alerted everyone there. Search parties went out and combed the countryside. Apparently, they spotted the blazing hut, but by then Dietrich and company had disappeared and we had gone with Liubov. When I returned the next day and told them what had happened, all search parties were brought in. Jim Stevens has a manhunt going for Dietrich and I hope they catch him."

Henri grinned, "They will…eventually. Liubov tells me the plan now is for me to stay with the Gypsies."

"Yes. Liubov thought of it, but even General Dayton thinks it's a good idea. Jim, Dayton and Dr. White rushed up here as soon as they learned where you were. They had a long conference with Liubov and he convinced them. The Nazis have gotten to you too many times while you were out in the open. With the Gypsies, no one can come near you without their knowing about it."

"That's true. Any stranger is looked upon with suspicion in a gypsy camp. They know their own and can see through a disguise instantly. Does my family know about the projected plan? What does my uncle think?"

"Yes, and they have agreed to it…somewhat reluctantly. I assured them you are in good hands and, above all, safe. Your uncle wants to send Igor up to stay with you. I talked with Liubov about it and he agrees. All we need is your okay."

"Great. Yes, I'd like to have him with me. Tell Uncle Paul to send him on and for him to bring some of my clothes with him."

"Will do. Oh, yes! Captain Harding doesn't know what to do with Vlaska. Apparently, he is raising hell at the stables."

Henri laughed. "That sounds like him. I would like to keep him with me, but he is too distinctive an animal. It would be like sending up a flare saying, 'Here I am.' When you talk with the family, ask them to send one of the grooms to fetch him."

"Right."

"By the way, how did you catch him?"

"He showed up at the stables on his own. Jimmy took hold of the bridle and led him into his stall. Jimmy said he was hungry."

"That also sounds like him. He always knows where he can get a good handout and will eventually show up there." Henri grinned. "There's a pub on the road, not too far from our place where we have stopped for a drink when we were out riding. The owner's daughter fell in love with Vlaska and always brought him some sugar and a pint of beer. One day, Vlaska was missing. We turned the country upside down looking for him. Eventually, we received a call from the pub owner to please come fetch our bloody horse. It seems Vlaska turned up, and after the daughter had given him his usual snack, he tried to follow her into the pub. Apparently, he was not very gentlemanly about it either."

Mario laughed, "Well, he apparently is not being a particularly gentlemanly guest at the stables either. The only one who can get near him is Jimmy. If anyone else tries, he lays his ears back and tries to bite them. I'll see to it he returns safely to the family fold."

"Thanks, Mario." Henri paused for a minute before saying, "You thought and acted fast the other night...you saved my life. Thank you."

Mario grinned and shrugged his shoulders, "No thanks necessary."

For the first time, Henri laughed. "*Touche*. Have you also planned how I am to get to the R.A.F. station for my flight to Nuremberg?"

"That has been worked out too. Liubov told us he would be near Fort William again at that time. He will send one of his sons to contact us. Jim and I know them by sight, so there will be no slip-ups there. When the time comes, we will pick you up from the camp."

"Right." Henri studied him for a few minutes before saying, "Why have you gone to all this trouble for me?"

Mario didn't answer at first, trying to marshal the reasons in the right order. Finally, he said, "Partly because I owe you my life twice over." When Henri raised a quizzical eyebrow, Mario digressed, "You didn't have to come back for me. You were in the clear, but you did anyway. Partly because when there was no love lost between us...Burt, Steve and I found out you were the one who influenced the general to not dismiss us from the Academy. He told us your reasons the day he called us in, after we got out of the hospital. Partly because I had an older brother, much like you. He had the same courage of conviction as you and was willing to lay down his life for what he believed in. I adored and worshipped him. He was beaten to death by the Nazis in a concentration camp after be bailed out of his plane. When I looked through the crack and saw what those bastards were doing to you, I made up my mind I would not leave you there alone in their hands. I…couldn't.

"I was not old enough to be in the army during the war, but if I can get back at them in any way at all, I will. Your testimony at the trial will hang three of them. By helping you get there, in a sense, I will be helping to hang them too." Mario paused, looking down at his hands while Henri watched him quietly. "And also I have discovered why such men as John Stanley, Larry Parker and Val Handly would walk through fire and hell for you." He shrugged his shoulders, embarrassed. "I don't know. Anyway, those are my reasons."

"Thank you, Mario. I hope I never let you down, but you have a great deal of courage and guts and the makings of an excellent officer. Do not sell yourself short. You could have slipped clear and come back with help at no risk to yourself. It took a lot, believe me I know, to do what you did, knowing if the plan backfired, you would be dead. You used your head and kept a cool one, and that was the most important thing."

Mario smiled. "Okay, enough said. Vance, Larry, John, Val and Pete wanted to come to see you too, but the general and Jim Stevens thought the less traveling between wherever you are camped and the Academy the better. Anyway, they said to say hello and wish you luck."

"Tell them the same from me and also tell them I'll write."

"Sure. I'd better go now. You look tired. Lita will have my neck. Liubov has invited me to stay overnight, so I'll see you in the morning before they strike camp."

"Again, thanks." Henri smiled. "Goodnight, Mario." He put his head back against the pillows with a sigh. The tenseness had gone out of his eyes. He relaxed completely and slowly fell asleep. He didn't hear Lita come back to curl up by his side.

The Gypsies broke camp the next day to move further north. All during the week, Henri remained in bed in the *vardo* while one of Liubov's sons drove the horse for Lita. Henri was becoming restless, but neither Lita nor Sonia would let him out of bed. Since they had hidden his clothes, he could do nothing about it. He tried to persuade the sons to bring them to him one night while Lita was fixing dinner, but they refused, drawing a finger across their throats to indicate what she would do to them. Wide grins spread across their faces, but they wouldn't budge.

Lita left the door open each night after supper when they camped so Henri could watch the life outside and hear the men softly sing the old Gypsy airs…the *mesalako dyila* and *pergetes* or play *khelimaske dylas*. Lita and Sonia removed his bandages every evening and washed and cleaned the wounds, then re-bandaged them. Henri slowly became accustomed to the routine of the camp and enjoyed the Gypsies, but with an underlying anxiousness to return to his own life.

One night after Sonia left, closing the door behind her, Lita sat curled up on the bed watching him. "You are hard, Boyar, hard as the stones outside on the ground," she commented finally. "You never flinch or make a sound when we change your bandages."

"There are two luxuries a Boyar is not allowed, my kitten…the luxury of cowardice and the luxury of giving in to pain"

"And yet you are soft and gentle when you make love, like a down pillow."

"A woman should not be treated as a cart horse, *maya galubka.*"

For a minute, he thought she was going to fight him. Then her tense body relaxed, molding into his. He felt her warm breath against his neck and knew he had won.

The next morning, when Henri awakened, his clothes hung neatly over a chair bringing a smile to his face. Lita brought him a steaming cup of coffee in an earthenware mug. He stretched his lean hard body luxuriously and sat up.

"The sun is bright today and we are to camp here until tomorrow," she said.

Henri sipped the hot liquid slowly, watching Lita move about the vardo, admiring her lithe grace and movement. Finally, he rose and dressed, including a white linen open necked shirt, slightly full in the sleeves, buttoning tight at the wrists. It was one such as a lot of the Gypsies wore. Sonia and Lita darkened his skin with juice from a berry so, from a distance, Henri was almost indistinguishable from the rest. Lastly, Lita tied a *diklo* around his neck.

"Good morning, your Highness, you are looking better. I trust you slept well last night," Liubov greeted him as Henri dropped lightly to the ground from the *Vardo*.

"Very well, thank you, Liubov," Henri answered with a smile. "You choose your campsites with an artistic eye."

The hills rose steeply around them and the small valley, covered in a misty haze of purple heather, lay beside a small lock, calm and cool under a pale blue sky. Bees hummed gathering the ingredients for their honey. The women washed clothes on flat stones by the lock or tended the fires and their cooking. The men mended harnesses or sat quietly on the steps of their *vardos* smoking. The older children scampered out to the meadow to tend the horses and the younger ones played amongst the *vardos*. Henri watched the quiet peaceful scene, sitting on the steps quietly talking with Liubov.

"I had heard of your family, but do not know much about them. We roamed much further south and west than where your lands lie."

Henri smiled to himself before explaining. Although Liubov had known Henri in the past, it had only been for a brief time. Henri knew that he was a special case. He realized the *Primas* wanted to know more abut him and his family now that he had been taken more intimately into their family. "We trace our line back to Rurick the Viking, about 862 A.D., partly by tradition, dating from that time, and partly by decree, the Bolkonsky clan has fought in the Tsar's armies, the Cavalry regiments. We have always had Cossacks on our land, and have always been taught by them to ride and fight. In recent times, the men of our family have led Cossack regiments into battle."

Liubov nodded silently. Henri looked curiously at him for a while. He wanted to ask a question that had been bothering him for some time now. "Why are you allowing me to live with Lita? She is your daughter, and I know that by the standards of most Gypsy families, this arrangement is not…uh, usual."

"It is not, Boyar, and I would not allow it with most men." Liubov pulled on his pipe sitting silently staring into the distance.

Henri began to think the Primas was not going to say anymore when suddenly he spoke again. "Lita's husband was killed not long ago in a knife fight. She is without a man and she is a woman who needs one. It will be hard to find another husband for her, one that can handle her, but in the meantime, you need a woman." Liubov shrugged his huge shoulders by way of finishing his explanation. He rose and looked down at Henri, smiling. "Tomorrow, we take a *nero drom*, a new road. We will meet your servant, Igor, at the end of the day. He can share the *vardo* with my sons."

Knowing fighting it would not make the time pass any faster, Henri contented himself wandering through the Scottish Highlands, enjoying the freedom and leisurely pace of the Gypsy's life. Those weeks he spent with them took on a dream-like quality, which he treasured. Accepted by the rest of the group, they invited him to sit by their campfires in the evenings. Sometimes during the day, when they traveled, he sat on the high seat with Lita close beside him, the reins loose in his hands, following Liubov's *vardo*. Sometimes, he walked beside the *vardo*, deep in his own thought. At such times, Lita watched him anxiously from the corners of her eyes, never interrupting his thoughts, sensing his need to be alone, and always greeting him with a brilliant smile when he climbed back up to the seat beside her. In the evenings, he sat with the others singing the lilting sad songs of the Russian Gypsies and forgetting his future and his past at night in Lita's arms. But the days of this free life were drawing to a close, his own last ordeal drawing near.

Chapter 15

Henri sat on the steps of the *vardo* that evening with Lita leaning against his legs. Little fires burned brightly, occasionally flaring up when a particularly dry branch caught. Their flickering lights played over the faces sitting around them, highlighting a cheekbone here, a bright eye there. The children slept, curled on the ground by their mothers' feet, and the jackals quietly dreamt under the *vardos*, the stars shining like diamonds in the blue/black backdrop of the sky. The sweet scent of grass and earth came to them on a light breeze. Now and then a horse whinnied softly. The soft strains of *gitari* and a *lavuta* floated across the clearing touching a chord deep within Henri. He sang softly, a sad Gypsy song of goodbye.

"You are sad, my Boyar," Lita turned her head to speak to him.

"This will be our last night together, *maya galubka*, and I am sad at the thought of parting." His eyes reflected his tender feelings for her. "But my ways are not your ways and I cannot remain with you forever."

Out of the darkness came another voice singing the refrain to the song. Henri rose silently and looked into the dying embers of their fire and taking Lita's hand, he led her into the *vardo*. The Gypsies continued to sing around their fires until nothing remained but the ashes.

Later that night, Henri's lean hard body relaxed, wrapped in the warm cocoon of darkness. Lita lay with her head pressed into the hollow of his neck, her arms lightly encircling him. They had been silent for some time when he felt her body begin to tremble. "What is the matter, *padruga*?"

"I am afraid," she whispered, "so terribly afraid. Something is going to happen. I can feel it and I am afraid."

147

Henri tightened his arms around her, stroking her hair. "Hush, *maya galubka*. There is nothing to fear. You are safe here with me."

"No...No!" She shivered again more violently. "I was dreaming, a *mulano*...a ghostly dream. I dreamt of the *mulesko chiriklo*. It is a bad omen."

"Hush, *tishe*." He kissed her softly, "It was only a bad dream. There is nothing to fear."

She didn't answer, but still he could feel her trembling. Suddenly, he tensed, his eyes narrowing slightly. His keen ears had picked up a stealthy sound somewhere near their *vardo* and he wondered briefly if she had heard it long before he had. Lita looked up at him. He moved her gently to one side, placing a finger across her lips, and then kissed them.

He moved to the curtained windows, pulling them back just enough to peer out. Five men stood in the center of the clearing. One man's back was turned away from Henri and the others appeared to be listening to him. Henri saw a movement from the window of Liubov's oldest son, Lonya. Lonya's face appeared and Henri motioned to him, pointing toward the clearing and holding up five fingers. Lonya nodded and disappeared.

Henri dressed quickly and slipped through the door like a shadow. Holding his *churi* in his hand, he moved to the back of the *vardo*, then darted across to Lonya's, where he made out the forms of Igor, Lonya and his brother, Sasha. The men in the clearing split up and moved toward some of the *vardos*.

Henri and his companions silently moved apart, each going toward a different one of the five men. Henri slipped under a *vardo*, using its wheel for cover. When the man he had chosen turned his back, Henri stealthily rose, and quietly coming up behind him, struck with the swiftness of a snake. He put one hand over his opponent's mouth and chopped him across the neck with the edge of his hand. The man slumped forward without a sound and Henri dragged him back out of sight. He bound and gagged him as Igor and the others silently and swiftly took care of their targets. Only one was left and Henri wanted that one for himself.

He moved to the center of the clearing, his cold deadly voice sounding loud in the still night air, "Were you looking for me, Dietrich?"

Henri threw his *churi* as Dietrich whirled, a gun glinting in his hand. Dietrich screamed as the blade pinned his arm against the side of the *vardo*. Sasha swiftly darted in, scooping up the gun and backing slowly away. Dietrich's scream had aroused the whole camp. Brush was heaped on the dying embers and the fires blazed up. The other four men were gathered up and placed under guard. No one went near Dietrich who remained pinned against the wall.

Henri did not move from where he was. His eyes held an unfathomable hatred. Loathing and revulsion for this creature who had so long been his enemy, mixed in his expression.

Liubov came up to his side and spoke quietly, "What are you going to do with this prisoner, Boyar?"

Henri didn't answer immediately. When he did, hate sparking from every word, it was not to Liubov. "What shall I do with you, Dietrich? Turn you over to the Gypsies to pass judgment? There is not a man amongst them that does not hate you. There is not a family here who would not dearly love to get their hands on you." Henri paused before going on, his voice icy. "Do you know who these people are? Gypsies, yes, but very special ones, Dietrich. Do you remember a little clearing in the woods just outside of Krakow? Do you remember one Christmas day in 1942 when you and your men decided to have a little sport with a group of wandering Gypsies you had rounded up? Do you remember that day? Or were there so many days like that you cannot remember this particular one?"

Dietrich nodded, his grey eyes coldly furious, as Henri went on. "This is what is left of that small band. You didn't know that, did you?" A hint of fear leaped in Dietrich's eyes as he shook his head. A vicious smile slipped across Henri's lips. "I thought not Shall I turn you over to them to torture you to death as you did their people? Or shall I turn you over to the Scottish authorities to be sent back to Nurenberg for trial?" He shook his head slightly, his eyes blazing. "Hanging is too quick…too clean a way for you to die, Dietrich."

He paused again, never taking his eyes from Dietrich's face. "Who has the most right to decide your fate? These people here? The men at Nuremberg? Or myself? I do not know the answer."

For the first time, Henri saw terror flickering in Dietrich's eyes. "No! I know you…your…your reputation. You cannot turn me over to these people. You are a humane person. For God's sake do not turn me over to them" Dietrich's voice had almost risen to a scream.

"Humane, Dietrich?" Henri savagely spat with rising fury. His face had taken on the hollow look of a skull whose eyes burned with a deadly fire. "What do you know of being humane? Were you humane when you tortured these people? Were you humane when you tried to hunt them down after they escaped? Were you humane when you butchered my family in a cellar in Dachau?" A cold deadly smile touched Henri's lips as sudden recognition showed in Dietrich's eyes. "Yes," Henri whispered softly, venomously, "I am the surviving member of that family, Dietrich. The one mistake you made…you let me live."

For a long moment more, Henri held Dietrich's eyes with his. He was afraid to let loose the emotions raging inside of him, so he held his body rigidly, leashing himself in, tightly, physically controlling his hatred for this man. If he did not, he knew he would kill Dietrich, blindly, unthinkingly. Turning abruptly away, afraid of himself if he remained any longer face to face with him, he snarled viciously over his shoulder, "I turn him over to you, Liubov, and to your people. You decide what to do with him. He is yours." Swiftly, he strode back to Lita's *vardo*, his ears ringing with Dietrich's terrorized pleas.

Henri knew the Gypsies would hold a council, for every one of them had a personal grudge against Dietrich. Henri sat on the bed, leaning his head against the wall, one leg stretched out. He held the knee of the other in tightly clasped hands, his knuckles turning white. The one man he hated with an undying passion, the man he had vowed to hunt down and kill, was out there within his grasp. The Gypsies would not betray him; he knew that. But did he have that right? The right to be judge, jury and executioner? All his training, beliefs and above all, his conscience revolted against the idea…that the arbitrary will of one man was the law. He had

150

fought against this ideology. His father had died fighting against it. In this ideology, no courts existed, no judges, no lawyers, no juries…only disappearances in the middle of the night; the mass deportations; the concentration camps; the mass murders. Henri knew he did not have the right to take the law into his own hands no matter what Dietrich had done to him, to his family, and to others. And so he forced himself to sit on the bed in the darkness of the *vardo*, for he didn't trust his own self-control; and because he did not trust himself, he had to turn Dietrich over to Liubov and his people, hoping they would make the right decision. The decision he knew he should make, feeling himself a coward for not doing so, and despising himself for it. He didn't know how long he sat there, his mind filled with memories, thoughts and torn emotions. Slowly, he became aware that Lita had lit the lamp and Liubov stood at his side.

As Henri silently looked up at him, Liubov said, "We have come to a decision." When Henri made no reply, he went on, "We have decided to turn him over to the Scottish authorities. Lonya has gone to the village to call them and Jim Stevens."

His eyes closed, Henri nodded his head. In a low strangled voice, he said, "You have done the right thing, Liubov."

"We decided that if we put him to death ourselves, no matter by what method, we would become like the animal he is. No better than the men who tortured and killed our people." Henri remained motionless as Liubov left without another word.

Lita turned out the light and silently sat down beside Henri, putting her arms around his neck. He pulled her to him and held her tightly, abstractedly stroking her hair until she fell asleep. He sat like a statue drained of all feeling, all emotion, until grey light started to show through the curtains. Only then did he close his eyes.

A dark grey mist hung heavily over Lock Ness. The men standing on the shore were barely able to see each other, although they stood in a close group. The horses, tethered to the trees behind them, snorted and chewed on their bits. The stamp of a hoof or the rattle of a chain became magnified in the milky stillness. No one had spoken for a while. Each man, wrapped in an ankle-length cloak, slowly paced the shoreline, straining his ears for the sound of oars. Other men, waiting in the forest on the hillside behind them, silently watchful, listened for any sound that might mean danger. Unseen hands lightly brushed the handles of gleaming, razor sharp *churis*, while drops of water fell from the trees like silent tears onto waiting shoulders.

Henri was the first to hear a muffled splash. He strained his eyes trying to pierce through the mist hiding the boat, following its progress with his ears until, like a wraith, it finally came into sight. A small beam flashed from a hooded torch and was answered by one in Liubov's hand.

"This is one hell of a night to pick for rowing across this loch," Jim remarked as he stepped from the boat, "...any loch for that matter! I expected to meet old Nessy any minute."

Henri grinned. "I don't think she likes nights like this any more than we do."

"Thank God for that. Everything is set on the other side." Jim turned to introduce the second man in the boat. "This is Francis McKay from our British counterparts. He and his men will be escorting us to the airfield. He also has the greatest stock of stories on meeting with Nessy and lighted phantom ships I have ever heard. I can't say that I have appreciated them tonight."

The two men shook hands; then Henri turned to Liubov. "Thank you again for everything you have done. I will never forget it."

Liubov smiled. "Come back and join us soon. You know you are always welcome." With that, he took Henri into his arms in a Russian hug. "*Ja develesa*, Boyar, *baht.*"

"*Ja develesa, Liubov, bahtalo drom.*"

Swiftly, Henri turned and stepped into the boat. Igor followed closely behind with Stevens and McKay. Quietly, they pulled away from shore and were swiftly swallowed by the mist. Blinded by it and having lost all sense of direction, Henri was astounded that McKay was able to steer the boat to the right spot on the other shore, but soon the stark jagged outlines of Castle Urquhart, standing on a promontory thrusting out into the black waters, appeared and they touched shore once more.

Moving with the silence of a cat, Henri skirted the cold damp stones, here and there covered with slippery moss, and started up the hill toward the road. The only sound to be heard was the soft breathing of the men; then a stone rolled under foot sounding like a small landslide in the stillness. Henri whirled, a knife suddenly appearing in his hand.

"Easy, Henri," Jim said in a low voice.

Henri slipped the knife back into his belt with a slight smile and continued walking quickly up the hill. When he caught sight of three cars parked off the road, he slowed his pace waiting for McKay to reach him. "Those are our people, Mr. Bolkonsky. Jim and I will ride with you in the lead car along with one of the best drivers we have, Bruce Lyam. The other two cars with four men in each are insurance, just in case of trouble."

"Right," Henri nodded, "Let's go." He settled back on the soft cushions of the Jaguar, with Igor and Jim on either side of him, as the small cavalcade of cars pulled onto the road.

Driving toward Fort William, the motor purred softly with Bruce's practiced hand on the wheel. Henri leaned his head back against the cushions and watched the road ahead through half-closed eyes, thinking about the end of his journey and the ordeal to come. The mist began to lift and he caught glimpses of the moon between high scudding black clouds. Lock Ness looked dark, forbidding and fathomless as the intermittent pale moonlight glinted on its mirrored surface.

Suddenly, McKay sat forward alert and suspicious. Henri's eyes sharpened. "What is it?"

"A car is coming up fast from behind and another is coming down the hill on that connecting road."

"Do you recognize either one?"

"No, but that's not surprising."

Bruce stepped on the accelerator and the Jaguar shot forward in instant response. "I'm going to try to get beyond the junction before they cut us off," he said, maneuvering the car around the sharp curves, pushing the speedometer higher and higher, squealing rubber screaming through the night, the darkness punctuated only by the light from the headlights bouncing crazily from tree to tree. The cars accompanying them sped up also, following closely, while the unknown car behind them attempted to catch up.

Jim reached inside his jacket, pulled out an automatic and checked its chamber, leaving the safety catch off. Igor, too, slipped a gun from his waist band.

McKay pulled a stengun from a secret compartment under the front seat, shouting above the roar of the powerful engine, "Normally, guns are forbidden, but this is a different game altogether." He grinned over his shoulder. "We received special permission. There are two more under your seat."

Jim leaned down and opened a compartment hauling out the guns. Checking the ammunition, he silently laid them on the floor by his feet. Henri watched all these preparations through half-slit eyes, a small sardonic smile playing about his lips. *They certainly came well prepared,* he thought. *I wonder how many guns are at the ready in the cars behind us?*

The Jaguar shot across the junction a fraction of a second before the car approaching on their right reached it. Jim leaned forward and looked out the window. He grunted then leaned back again in his seat.

A buzzer sounded on a radio set in the front seat. McKay clicked a switch saying tersely, "McKay here."

Crackling came from the receiver before they heard a clipped British voice, "The other two sets of cars we sent ahead as decoys have been attacked, but no one was seriously hurt. Unfortunately, four of the cars are out of commission. Do you have a map?"

"Yes." McKay took a map from his jacket pocket and spread it on his knees.

"They've set up a roadblock at the junction with the road to Gairlochy, just before Spean Bridge. There's no road off this main one to get around them."

"Right. I have it pinpointed," McKay said.

"Try to bowl through them. We're coming up from Fort William and will join you as soon as we can."

"Roger. Over and out." McKay snapped off the set and sat back. "Do your best, Bruce."

The driver merely nodded his head, not taking his eyes from the road. As they slid around a bend, two cars blocked the road where they had to turn left. Bruce pressed down on the accelerator. It looked as if he were going to smash right through them. At the last moment, he swerved over a grass verge, climbed a small hill with another burst of speed and spun out onto the road to Spean Bridge. Bursts of gunfire followed them. Henri looked back. Only one of their cars had made it around the road block; the other rested on its roof, its wheels spinning helplessly in the air. The good news was that it effectively blocked other cars from pursuing them, gaining them a little time...not much...but for a driver like Bruce, it would have been enough...except that as they raced away, they heard an ominous thump...thump...thump.

Bruce quickly pulled over to the side and leaped out of the car. McKay activated the radio as Henri reached down and picked up one of the stenguns, but McKay's hand on his arm stopped him from getting out of the car. "Stay here and keep out of the way. You'll only get hurt, and my people will have my neck if that happens, to say nothing of yours."

"I don't like being trapped anywhere. Besides, I know how to use one of these." He slipped out crouching down behind the car.

Bruce had pulled off the road on the inside of the curve, which gave them some advantage. As the second car pulled up behind them, everyone piled out. McKay finished his call to the cars coming to meet them and knelt beside Henri. The two cars provided the only real cover available, except for a drainage ditch on the other side of the road. Henri, Jim and Igor ran across dropped into it and waited tensely for their pursuers to appear.

Henri heard the cars coming and nudged Jim. The three men flattened themselves deep into the ditch. The first car sped around the curve. Its driver didn't see the two parked cars in time and a murderous crossfire sent it spinning drunkenly into a field behind, where it burst into flames. The second car, close on the heels of the first, was able to stop before coming parallel. The men in the car tried taking pot shots out the window, but a few well-placed bullets in the petrol tank made them scramble out of the car, while the remaining two cars pulled up short, tires squealing, sparks flying and then silence.

McKay slipped quickly across the road. "Our other car is still in working condition, Mr.Bolkonsky. I suggest we use it to get out of here."

"But there are nine of us; if we all squeeze in there will be no room for the driver to maneuver."

"We'll leave four men here to cover us."

"Four against ten!" Henri raised an eyebrow. "Those odds are not cricket."

"Cricket or not, you have to get out of here!"

"No. We'll all stay until your reinforcements arrive." Henri moved up the road using the ditch for cover, before McKay could protest further.

Henri, Jim, Igor and McKay slowly worked their way around the curve. Peering over the edge of the ditch, they were surprised to see only one man near the two parked cars. Glancing up, Henri spotted the outlines of their pursuers working their way up the small hill in an attempt to get above and behind McKay's men.

Henri crawled from the ditch and raced across the road. Pulling out his knife, he slashed the tires on the vehicles and, making sure Jim and Igor were covered, he opened fire up the hill. McKay raced back along the ditch to warn Bruce and the others and bring them back with him around the curve.

Bullets kicked up the dirt, ricocheted off the cars and macadam sending up showers of rock and dust. A sudden silence felt almost as loud as the battle had been. Henri looked around. "Is everyone all right?"

McKay checked and found that only one of his men had been wounded, and only slightly. "It looks like it." The roar of motors sprang up out of the silence. "Duck for cover!" he yelled, but Bruce called out, "It's all right; they're our people." Their small grim group split up, climbing into the welcome vehicles.

Henri leaned back against comfortable cushions once more, closing his eyes until the gates to the airfield loomed ahead. "Thank you for your help, Mr. McKay. I sincerely appreciate it…and Bruce's driving," he added with a grin.

"It's been a pleasure meeting you, Mr. Bolkonsky, and thanks for your help back there. If you ever need a job, you know where to find me." McKay grinned back.

"I'll remember that."

His family waited for Henri at the airfield and with a last handshake for McKay, they all climbed aboard the air force plane for the last leg of his journey to the Continent, and one last unfinished part of his war.

Chapter 16

Henri didn't want anyone in his family to hear his testimony, hoping to shield them from knowing the full story of what had happened to his parents. He argued vehemently with Paul. They finally agreed that the women should not go to the trial, but Paul insisted on being there, if for no other reason than to lend Henri his support when it was over. Alexei and Jean also insisted on going in order to be with both Henri and Paul if they needed them. Henri could do nothing to dissuade them and finally completely withdrew into himself for the rest of the flight to Nuremberg. Alicia, Maria, and Carlotta went on to the Schloss with Pyotr. Igor drove to the courthouse and waited outside with the car.

Paul, Alexei and Jean left Henri at the door to the witness room. Entering the visitor's section, they found the courtroom relatively empty. All the "big fish" had been sentenced and now only the "small fry" were left. They easily found seats together in the front where they had a good view of the room.

The judges' bench stood raised on a dais with eight chairs beneath the flags of their respective nations, waiting for their occupants. The prosecution attorneys' tables stood in front, a little lower down. A film screen covered one wall with the witness stand in front of it. Opposite, a table stood with several canisters of film. Windows high up in the wall shed a dim light over the courtroom as the lights along the wall and hanging from the ceiling had not been turned on.

A few more people came in to sit near the Bolkonskys, arranging themselves comfortably before the proceedings, their chairs creaking loudly as they did. Three attorneys entered talking quietly amongst themselves. They arranged their papers and files on the tables. The door of the lift opened and a stir moved through the room as three prisoners with their guards emerged from the door of the lift and walked to their places in the dock.

Paul stared at them, knowing these men had tortured and killed his brother and his family, and wondered why he did not feel anything at all. Neither anger nor hatred stirred in him...only a detached curiosity such as a scientist would have looking through a microscope at some new strange microbe.

The noise level in the courtroom gradually rose as more people entered, reminding Jean of an orchestra slowly assembling to tune their instruments before a performance. Each man went to his allotted place; some with serious demeanors; others exchanging quips; papers rustled as attorneys and their assistants drew them from their briefcases and arranged them in neat piles on the tables; chairs scraped and creaked; a throat rasped, clearing; a hand raised in greeting to a friend; knowing looks exchanged; a smile; the well oiled machinery of a court in session caught the eyes and ears of those watching.

All the attorneys were present, the translators, the court reporters and the inevitable newspaper reporters, most of whom looked bored, believing no really sensational revelation would come out anymore to capture the headlines. Horror had been piled upon horror to the point where the public had become surfeited and were no longer shocked. It was almost as if they had been numbed and now their emotions could no longer react to the hideous cruelties perpetrated on innocent people.

Everyone rose as the judges entered and took their places on the bench. The indictments had been read and the opening statements had been made the preceding day. Now the American attorney rose to call the first witness against the accused. Paul, Alexei and Jean leaned slightly forward in their seats as Henri appeared at the door from the witness room. He walked quietly to his place and in a low steady voice took his oath.

His bearing and manner seemed remote, even cold, but Paul knew he was wired like a time bomb, steeling himself to face this court and unlock the door to a memory he had tried to erase.

Henri stood resting his hands lightly on the rail in front of him, his face a mask, pale under his tan. He held his body rigidly straight, his eyes dark and slightly narrowed as he glanced briefly

159

at the three men with their guards. He allowed his face to betray none of the emotions raging through him.

Following the preliminary questions, the attorney for the prosecution said, "Mr. Bolkonsky, will you tell this court what happened to your family in the spring of 1938?"

Henri took a deep breath and gave a short background to the events leading up to Dachau. "My father, Stephen Edourdovich Bolkonsky, was a professor of Political Science at the University of Berlin. He had held that post for five years. All during that time, he had spoken out against Fascism and Hitler. Several times during this period, he had been threatened, but being the man he was, refused to stop his opposition publicly or privately. Early in the year, I believe sometime in late January or early February, he was relieved of his post. We stayed on in Berlin; partly because my father felt a responsibility to his students, many of whom still came to the house to visit; partly because many of his German friends who were opposed to Hitler, felt Father might be able to use his influence with various governments to stop Hitler's projected aggressions. In his conversations with all of them, he continued to speak out against Hitler and his ideas."

Henri's voice took on a grating edge as he proceeded. "One night in late April, the S.S. came to our house and arrested my father. Mother tried to find out where he was, but to no avail. A week later, they came again. This time they took the whole family, except my sister Maria, who was three-months-old at the time. First, we were taken to their headquarters in Berlin. The next day, we were transported to Dachau and put in separate cells. That night and part of the next day, the S.S. took us one by one from our cells to be questioned. Finally that evening, they herded us together in the basement of the building where we saw my father."

Up to this point, Henri's voice was low, but steady. Now he gripped the rail in front of him and with seeming difficulty continued, "At first, we did not recognize Father...he had been tortured so badly. Up to a point, we had been also, but our treatment was mild compared to what they had done to him. I don't believe an unbroken bone remained in his body. Mother cried out and tried to go to him, but one roughly knocked her back with the butt of his rifle...They tied all of us to posts set in the floor then…proceeded to…strip my mother. After…after they…raped her…they tied her to a wooden plank…then opened an oven door and slowly…feet first…fed…her to the flames…while she was still alive." Henri paused, his face now deathly pale. "This process of rape…and…and…burning was repeated with my two older sisters and my two older brothers…After that…they did the same with my father…To this day, I do not know why they didn't kill me with the rest of my family." Henri's voice trailed off into a whisper; a muscle twitched spasmodically in his jaw. The far away look that had dropped over his eyes remained even after he finished speaking.

One day, when he had lost his temper, Henri had shouted out an extremely short account of the event to Paul. Now, as Paul sat horrified at the fuller account, he realized why Henri had tried so hard to persuade him not to come. Alexei silently laid his hand on his father's arm, glancing anxiously between Henri and Paul, thinking if he had known the full story, he would have sided with Henri to prevent his father from coming.

Paul, startled…brought back to the present by the voice of the prosecution attorney. "Thank you, Mr. Bolkonsky. We would like you to watch a film and tell us if you recognize any of the people in it."

The defense attorneys immediately leaped up, objecting to the introduction of the film and a heated argument ensued. This gave Henri time to collect himself, for his mind had become locked away from those around him. Now he caught the tail end of the argument and realized, with sick horror, what the film was about. The judges consulted together and decided to overrule the objection, allowing the film to be admitted into evidence.

Desperately, Henri turned toward them. "Your Honors, is it absolutely necessary for me to see the film?"

"We believe it is, as you must identify the people in it, Mr. Bolkonsky," the American judge answered, adding, "We understand your reluctance and we are sorry to have to make you go through this ordeal, but it is necessary."

Henri wanted to scream, *No! I lived through it once. I cannot do it again,* but he remained silent, the scream dying in his throat, but reaching his eyes. He glanced with unfathomable

161

anguish toward Paul as the lights dimmed. After the first few feet, Henri bowed his head unable to bring himself to watch. Leaning heavily on the rail for support, he waited until the lights came up again.

Paul leaned forward in his chair, his elbows on his knees, his hands covering his face. Alexei and Jean, their faces ashen, placed their arms around his shoulders trying to comfort him. Paul looked up to find Henri's eyes on him. It was all he could do to keep from leaping the barrier and going to him. He wanted to put his arms around Henri and lead him from the courtroom. His own anguished heart went out to his nephew who had been through so much already and had to watch his family tortured and killed…not once but twice. He tried to tell Henri with his eyes how he felt, hoping his nephew would understand.

"We are sorry to have to put you through this, but were the people in the film your family, Mr. Bolkonsky?" the prosecution attorney asked, breaking the silence.

"Yes," he whispered.

"And the men standing accused are three of the five who were in the film and who murdered your family?"

"Yes."

"Thank you, Mr. Bolkonsky. I have no further questions."

The American judge spoke, "Do you wish to cross-examine, Herr Werneke?"

One of the defense attorneys cleared his throat and rising, looked directly at Henri. His grey hair, white at the temples, pale grey tailored suit with a pearl grey tie, matched the steel grey of his eyes. Snow-white French-cuffs showed just the right amount below the sleeve of his jacket and, Alexei thought, inconsequentially, his shoes were probably black with a high gleaming polish. The timbre of his voice was that of an actor, as all good trial attorneys must be able to shade and color the meaning of every word. It was polite, but with a hint of sarcasm behind it as he asked, "It seems to me you have a remarkable memory for events and actions which you say happened over ten years ago, Mr. Bolkonsky. Can you explain this phenomena, other than the events were so terrible that they impressed themselves on your mind?"

"I happen to have a photographic memory," Henri replied, "with total recall."

"I see." Picking up a book, seemingly at random, from the table, the attorney asked, "Would you mind proving it?"

A small sardonic smile flitted across Henri's lips as he inclined his head slightly, "As you wish."

"Let the record show, the book is American Jurisprudence by A.J. Black, opened at page two-hundred-thirty."

Henri took the book, quickly read the page indicated, handed it back and repeated, word for word, what he had read.

"Thank you, Mr. Bolkonsky." Obviously not having expected that result, the attorney hesitated and then continued, "Now, the men in the film and the men standing accused...you say are the same, yet I can see quite a few differences. Can you explain this?"

"They are ten years older, but their features have not changed other than a few more lines. I will admit two of them have grown fatter since then, but that still does not alter the fact they are the same men."

"You have changed a great deal in that time, Mr. Bolkonsky."

"Yes, but thirteen-year-old boys do. Grown men do not," he shot back.

The attorney had no argument for this and changed his tack, "Mr. Bolkonsky, you hate the men who murdered your family, do you not?"

The prosecution attorney immediately leaped to his feet, "I object to this line of questioning, your Honors, as it can fruitlessly lead nowhere."

Again a heated argument began, ending in the judges' decision to allow the question. Paul, watching Henri, knew he was keeping himself under control with a tremendous effort. He was afraid the time bomb would explode and he had no idea what would happen then.

"Yes, of course," Henri answered, "would you not feel hatred too?"

"And you hate all Nazis, since all Nazis represent these men to you, is that not so, Mr. Bolkonsky?"

"Your Honors. This is ridiculous and a waste of time. All these questions are in the realm of speculation!" the prosecuting attorney cut in.

"Your Honors, these questions are not, as my colleague says, 'in the realm of speculation,' but a very real possible basis for the witness' motivation in pointing these men out as the murderers of his family."

Again, the objection was overruled and the question was asked again. "To some extent, but I hate the ideology of Fascism more."

"Are you not then blinded by this into wanting to take your revenge on the three men standing here today? After all they were Nazis and members of the S.S. admittedly, but could you not be mistaken in your identification?"

"I cannot be mistaken, sir," Henri replied, his eyes flashing. "As far as taking my revenge, as you call it, against the Nazis, I have already done so and I believe my record will prove that."

Try as he would, the attorney could not shake Henri's conviction nor make him say anything that would indicate he had any doubt in his mind. After a half hour of questioning, he gave up and changed tactics once more. Moving some papers on the table in front of him, he appeared to study them for a moment. "Is it not true, Mr. Bolkonsky that your father was made an Honorary member of the S.S.?"

"Yes, but…"

Cutting in before Henri had a chance to finish, he said in an extremely reasonable voice, "Does it not seem strange then, that if he preached as hard as you say he did against Hitler, that one of Hitler's right hand men, Himmler in fact, would give him a membership in the 'Elite Corps'?"

"My father refused the membership. He would have nothing to do with it." Henri's voice remained calm, but with an unmistakable edge to it.

"Why was it offered in the first place?"

"Because my father was an influential man and had many friends and connections all over the world. They wanted to use him for their own ends. That is why it was offered and also why he was allowed to live so long."

Again, the attorney paused, studying Henri before saying with the air of dropping a bomb, "Does the name Heinrich von Spieldau mean anything to you?"

"Yes, of course."

"Would you tell the court in what connection?"

"It was one of the names I used during the war."

"I see. You were a commissioned officer of the Wehrmacht under that name, were you not, Mr. Bolkonsky?"

"I held the rank of Lieutenant and later Captain under that name, yes, but…"

Again, the attorney interrupted, "You also were awarded the Iron Cross and were decorated by Hitler himself."

"I was but…"

Werneke let a slight hint of exasperation enter his tone. "Just answer the question, Mr. Bolkonsky. Were you or were you not awarded the Iron Cross?"

Henri's temper was beginning to fray and his eyes flashed. "Yes, but…"

Sharply, the attorney interrupted again, "Were you or were you not decorated by Hitler himself…yes or no…Mr. Bolkonsky?"

"Yes."

"At the same time, you were appointed Aide to General von Graf, were you not?"

Henri, knowing what the attorney was trying to do, wanted to shout furiously at him, but abruptly, reined in his temper, answering quietly, "Yes."

"And you held the post until the end of the war, did you not?"

"Yes."

"Is your testimony a little like the pot calling the kettle black, Mr. Bolkonsky?"

"No!"

"The Wehrmacht's hands are not that clean, Mr. Bolkonsky, and you of all people, knew what was going on."

"Yes, I knew what was happening in the concentration camps. I certainly do not deny that."

"And yet, you became an officer, were decorated and remained in the German Army until the end of the war."

165

"I was under orders to do so."

Werneke showed surprise mixed with sarcasm. "Whose orders? You certainly were not ordered to act so bravely as to be awarded the Iron Cross!"

"That was pure accident." Henri's voice turned cold and hard.

"The Iron Cross is not awarded by 'pure accident,' Mr. Bolkonsky."

"This one was." Henri again checked his anger quickly before going on in the tone of an adult explaining something to a child. "If we had not held up the advance of the Russian spearhead as we did, I would have been captured and/or killed by the Russians and that would have done British Intelligence absolutely no good at all."

"British Intelligence?" Werneke pounced. "You hold an American Passport. This happened before the Americans entered the war and before you worked for them?" The tone of his voice showed disbelief in Henri's last statement.

"I originally worked for M16 and was trained by them."

"You tell a strange tale to say the least, Mr. Bolkonsky. You would have this court believe that you worked for British Intelligence, yet carry an American Passport; were awarded the Iron Cross by, and I quote, 'pure accident;' were a Captain in the Wehrmacht and an aide to one of their top generals, and you also want this court to believe your earlier testimony that you hate Fascism, the Nazis and all they stand for? I find this hardly credible!" Abruptly, the prosecution attorney dismissed him with a thinly veiled sneer. "No more questions."

The American attorney stood. "Mr. Bolkonsky, where were you in 1940?"

Oh! God. How long is this going to keep up? It's as if I were on trial, not the S.S. He answered quietly, "In France."

"You were there when the German army marched in?"

"Yes."

"What did you do at that time?"

"I formed a resistance group and went underground."

Slowly, step-by-step, the prosecution lawyer took Henri through his actions and work during the war. Almost numb, Henri answered the questions through a haze of tiredness. Paul, Alexei and Jean were beside themselves with anger. It was bad enough for them, but Henri was far more emotionally involved.

Finally, the prosecution attorney finished his last group of questions. "Since my colleague has made such a point of your being decorated with the Iron Cross, I believe, Mr. Bolkonsky, you have also been decorated by the French Government with the Croix de Guerre, the Cross of Lorraine and the Legion of Honour. Is this not so?"

"Yes."

"You have also been decorated by the British Government with a Distinguished Service Order and Order of the British Empire?"

"Yes."

"And by the American Government with a Distinguished Service Cross?"

"Yes."

"Thank you. Mr. Bolkonsky, I believe that is all."

The American judge leaned forward. "Thank you for your cooperation with this court, Mr. Bolkonsky. Again, we are sorry to have had to put you through this trying experience. You may step down now."

Henri heard the judge as if from a distance. He quietly bowed to the judges, turned and left the courtroom. In the witness room, he grabbed the back of a chair for support and stared unseeing into the middle distance. Silent tears flowed down his cheeks, his body shook violently. He tightened his grip on the chair to prevent his legs from buckling under him and leaving him a heap on the floor.

The door opened and a guard looked in. "Mr. Bolkonsky, your family is waiting for you."

Henri raised his head with unseeing eyes and vaguely nodded. Calling upon the self-discipline he had been taught from childhood, he released his hold on the chair and walked blindly through the door into the hallway. He stopped and stood still, unable to move toward Paul, who stood a little way from him. Slowly, brokenly, he said, "I...I'm sorry, Uncle Paul. I...had...no idea a…film…existed." His voice dropped to a horrified whisper. "I didn't know."

Paul reached him in two strides and held him in his arms. Henri dropped his head on Paul's shoulder. Holding onto his uncle, he buried his face. Paul could feel Henri's body trembling as he fought for control. Holding his nephew more tightly, he whispered, "My God! Henri." Words were useless at this time and his own voice broke as he said, "Damn it, my son, cry." Fiercely his arms formed a protective ring around Henri, his own tears falling silently down his cheeks. Paul cried for his brother whom he had loved, for the family that had been lost, and for the heartbreak and anguish of his nephew. The two men stood for a time with Alexei and Jean shielding them from curious eyes.

Henri raised his head and gently pulled away from Paul. "Thank you." The two simple words expressed a world of meaning. "Come on, let's get out of here."

Epilogue

Ladislaus and Henri stretched out on chaise lounges under a tree in the garden after a merry, but boisterous, lunch with two sturdy little children at the table. Now, Henri could hear Mary trying to put them down for their naps. Shouts, squeals and laughter came hurtling through the open windows. Ladislaus and Henri smiled as they followed the progress of the battle.

Warm sun dappled through the leaves of the trees, patterning their bodies in ever shifting lights. Bees hummed drowsily amongst the flowers neatly planted in their beds and the smell of new mown grass mingled with the scent of roses. From time to time, the mooing of a cow could be heard from a distant field, or a bird calling to another.

Henri had arrived the evening before and the two men had talked until the early morning hours, catching up on each other's lives. Now they sat in companionable silence, not wanting to disturb the quiet afternoon. A lovely tall blond woman appeared at the doorway, her long slim brown legs moving in a springy walk across the sloping lawn. Her blue eyes laughed as she came up to the men, throwing herself on an empty chaise. "Those two are so excited, I didn't think I would ever get them down."

"From the silence, I would say you succeeded admirably, Mary," Henri said smiling.

"Would either of you like a refill on your drinks?"

"Stay where you are. I'll get them," Ladislaus said, rising and taking Henri's glass. "Anything for you, sweetheart?"

She shook her head.

"That godson of mine is growing into quite a boy," Henri remarked.

"Yes, and he's more like his father everyday." Mary laughed. "He starts jumping lessons this fall; did you know? He's turning out to be quite a rider."

"Well, he's old enough now." Henri's sharp ears caught the sound of the telephone and noticed that Mary had too.

A shadow passed across her normally smiling face, but was gone almost instantly. "That's what his father said. I do believe you two were poured out of the same mold, you think so much alike."

Henri answered with a laugh. "We had much the same training, though in different parts of the world and we both fell in love with the same girl."

"You've changed, Henri," she remarked as she studied his face, her head cocked slightly to one side.

"Oh! In what way?" Henri raised one eyebrow.

"I don't know. You seem to be freer, more light-hearted, as if a cloud has lifted from over your head."

"You are very perceptive, my luv." He laughed again. "Perhaps. I admit I have chased away some demons recently." He looked up as Ladislaus appeared at the door of the house with freshly made drinks.

Ladislaus carried the tray across the lawn. Henri watched, his eyes searching his friend's face for some clue. "That was Jan on the telephone, Henri. He wanted to know if you had any relatives still in Russia."

"Yes, I believe so. As far as I can remember, there are two sons by a distant cousin still there, but I don't know if they're still alive."

Ladislaus paused. "How much have you guessed about what is going on?" he asked.

"You're leading, or rather commanding, an underground railroad in connection with a resistance group in Hungary. Jan and Yurick are in on it too."

Ladislaus nodded his head, smiling slightly. "You are far too quick, Henri. You're right. I am. Some of the men who were with me in the mountains are still in Hungary. We have a way to pass messages and so forth, back and forth, and to help those who wish to escape or who have to escape." He paused a second before

170

continuing. "Jan has learned that a young man, who looks enough like you to be your twin brother, was captured by the KGB trying to escape across the border about a week ago in Buda-Pesht."

Henri's eyes narrowed as he watched Ladislaus closely. "It could be my cousin; I don't know."

"We'll try to find out what happened to him and who he is exactly. We may never know, of course."

"Uncle Paul has been trying to trace the cousins for a long time. This will be one more piece of information for him."

"What would you do if you did find them?"

Henri shrugged. "Go in and try to get them out, if they wanted to come out."

"That's what I thought. You're a mad fool, Henri, and bloody reckless." Ladislaus laughed. "That's the sort of wild escapade you'd enjoy. All right. But if you ever do seriously contemplate anything of the sort, contact me and I'll put you in touch with people in Hungary, Poland and Russia who will help you."

Henri grinned. "Right. I promise." He lifted his head to listen. "I think that's Igor coming to fetch me. I'm sorry I can't stay longer, but perhaps when I return…"

The two men rose and walked around the house with Mary between them. When they reached the front, Henri bent down and kissed her on the forehead. "Goodbye, my love, and take good care of my godson. Don't let him break his neck on the first jump."

"I will and take care of yourself, Henri. The next time you come, stay longer."

Henri and Ladislaus stood for a long moment in silence, neither wanting to say goodbye. Finally, Henri said, "Take care of yourself and remember, if you need me for anything, even a hair-brained scheme, I'll be here."

"I'll remember, Henri. Watch out for yourself too and stop risking your neck so quickly. We need you in this world not the next."

Henri stood with his hand on the car door and now, with a last grin, he slipped into the seat beside Igor, who put the car in gear. Henri waved to Ladislaus standing with his arm around

171

Mary, both of whom smiled with a touch of sadness, until the car disappeared around a bend and was lost to sight.

With a sigh, Henri turned his thoughts elsewhere, toward home and, perhaps, a quieter more peaceful life. Smiling ruefully he shook his head, *It's a nice dream, but not one that will likely ever come to pass.*

DIANA HARNED
1933 - 2005

Diana Harned, writing as D. Forrester Newhall, was born and raised in San Francisco. After graduating from Sarah Dix Hamlin School, she attended San Mateo College, majoring in English and History. She lived in Europe with her husband for fourteen years traveling extensively throughout Europe as well as Greece, Egypt, India, Nepal, Thailand, Singapore and Hong Kong. While living in England, she wrote a number of articles on Sighthounds, Coursing and Lure-Coursing, which were published in various English dog magazines and she trained, showed and hunted with Borzoi for almost forty years. She belonged to the Penman Club and the London Writers Circle in England and to The Villages Creative Writing Group in The Villages, Florida for several years before her untimely death.

Diana's daughters, Jacqueline Harned and Jeannine Harned Smith were born during her years in Europe. Retiring to Florida, she shared her home with her beloved Borzoi, Storm.

Her first two books, in the Henri Bolkonsky series, *The Spider's Web* and *The Hunt is Away* will soon be reissued, and the last book in the series, *Escape from the Gulag*, will be published posthumously, following this edition of *Black Horse, Black Rider*.

173

The first two novels in the Henri Bolkonsky trilogy are available:

The Hunt is Away
Divided Vienna
www.amazon.com

The Spider's Web
Occupation of Nazi Germany
www.booksbyjoan.com
(an imprint of www.firesidepubs.com)

www.ingramcontent.com/pod-product-compliance
Lightning Source LLC
Chambersburg PA
CBHW070920130626
46555CB00001B/221